The
Country
Doctor

Jean McConnell

Previously published in
serialised form as *Linda Ford, Locum*
and in Large Print as *The Substitute Doctor*

ISBN: 978-1909752122
ISBN-13: 1909752126

CHAPTER ONE

THE CIDER ORCHARD

My territory!

Linda Ford stopped her car on the hill, got out and leant over a gate staring across the field that sloped down into a maze of orchards and away in a pattern of lush green, yellow and dark red that typifies the western counties of England.

I'm a country doctor now, she thought. It wasn't what she'd had in mind when she made the great decision at grammar school in London – half expecting to be laughed to scorn; when she'd tentatively mentioned that she wanted to study medicine and been amazed to find that they thought she might try. At that time her ambition had soared.

Linda Ford the new Madame Curie! Shaking the world with a great breakthrough in medical knowledge!

Her parents had hardly subscribed to this dream. In fact it had taken some time to convince them that their wild young daughter was contemplating anything so at variance with the evidence of her bedroom – that confusion of colourful pin-ups, scattered homework notes and non-stop pop. Their only daughter, who was so slapdash when she helped them in their little dairy on Saturdays – yet knew the name of every customer. They continued in a state of astonishment, although so consumed with pride in her endeavours, that Linda became shy of giving a hand in the dairy, knowing that all the regulars were being supplied with a blow-by-blow account of her examination struggle.

By the time she had passed her finals and taken her place amongst the junior doctors in a teaching hospital they accepted that she really was a budding medical genius.

But Linda was perplexed to find her interest in research fading. The reason only became crystalised one day when a patient in a geriatric ward took her hand and said: 'You make me feel you care about me, dear.' 'I do!' Linda had replied, and realised in that moment that it was not medicine in the abstract, not experiments in laboratories she wanted, but contact with complex, contrary, aggravating, fascinating human beings.

She was happy working in hospital for a year, walking the wards. Blissful in fact, for someone very special to her was walking beside her.

Then the pattern changed. Suddenly she found herself walking alone. She'd been so sure they were right for each other. Felt so secure. Been so secure. Been so deeply committed.

It was painful and bewildering; and she'd run two hundred miles away and plunged into a job she'd hardly had time to consider. For the next six months she was to be locum to a Doctor John Cooper, whose partner had died suddenly, in a practice in the West Country.

But with every fresh morning she brightened. With every drive through the sweet air she found herself reviving.

And there were people here a-plenty – relying on her judgement – putting their faith in her decisions. It was a little alarming. But it was a challenge and certainly drove depressing memories from the mind.

Linda stood gazing over the orchards, feeling the sun warm on her face, then she climbed back into the little M.G. and drove on.

Across the valley, a woman was picking her way through those orchards. In the distance just a toy figure. A busy, searching figure that turned this way and that like a distracted ant, then came to a dead stop in the long grass.

The sudden scream alarmed a flock of sparrows from the laden apple boughs.

Mrs Danbury ran, wildly zig-zagging through the orderly ranks of trees, into the back gate of her cottage.

'Dicker! Come quick!'

Her son hastily latched the hutch-door on his pet ferret and hurried to her. She clutched at his shirtsleeve.

'It's Betty! I've just found her in the orchard – lying in the grass. Get out your bike and fetch the doctor! Ride up to Whitelaws – they'll telephone for you. And hurry! I can't move the girl!'

The closed-circuit radio in the car bleeped at Linda as she was driving down a narrow lane. She eased off and answered.

'Dr Ford?' said the voice from the surgery.

'Yes?' said Linda.

'We've had a call from Mrs Danbury. Her daughter's been found unconscious. It's Roseberry Cottage – the other side of Mead Orchards.'

'Can you just give me some directions, Mrs Perry? Right now I'm about three miles north of Pretting.'

Linda thought she heard a faint sigh. It wasn't such an unreasonable request. Six weeks was hardly time enough to get familiar with the area. Linda had not realised how widely scattered a rural practice could be.

Trudging knee-deep in mire on a dark night was no joke. Nor winding round endless lanes that all looked alike to her town eyes.

On her first trip into Yelchester she'd bought wellingtons, a sou'wester and a compass!

Mrs Perry's flat voice, giving detailed directions, came to a halt. Linda thanked her and switched off.

She's an efficient woman, thought Linda, and she's been Doctor Cooper's receptionist for many years. I suppose I was a bit of a surprise, but she'll get used to me.

The same could be said for the patients, as Linda had demonstrated to her a little later when she got to Roseberry Cottage.

'It's not the proper doctor, Ma. It's that girl.' Dick Danbury turned, realised that Linda had come up behind him, and went scarlet. His mother glared at him, and beckoned Linda inside.

'My daughter's on the sofa, Doctor. Old Tom helped me lug her in.'

Betty Danbury looked up at Linda with a bewildered smile.

'I suddenly come over queer,' she said.

'Come over queer!' snorted Mrs Danbury. 'If she won't tell you what happened I will! I warned her to keep clear of that man!'

'Ma, don't!'

But as Linda began a quiet examination of the girl, her mother chattered on angrily.

'Foster, it is. The chap that's taken over these orchards. Always hanging around by here. I told Betty to watch out but she would cut across just to save a few minutes.'

'I tell you nothing like that happened, Ma!'

'Oh? Then where did you get those marks then?'

Linda frowned over the red patches inside the girl's wrists and down her face and neck.

'I must've fallen in some nettles. I'm all right now, honestly Doctor, and it's time I fed the baby.'

'Baby?' queried Linda. 'How old is it?'

'Eight weeks.'

'You stay there, my girl. I'll get the bottle. You've had a bad shock.' Mrs Danbury bustled out of the room.

'*Were* you attacked?' asked Linda.

Betty shook her head. Her blue eyes were guileless. She seemed quite recovered, except for the weals.

'I'll give you something to cool those down,' said Linda and wrote a prescription. 'And have you been well since the birth of the baby?'

'Oh yes. Doctor Cooper looked after me so everything was fine.'

One day, perhaps, *I'll* earn such warm confidence, thought Linda.

The fainting fit Linda attributed to postnatal weakness and the hot day, but Mrs Danbury was not to be moved from her own theory.

'Don't you believe my Betty. Always a close one, she's been, and never liked to get anyone into trouble. But it was Foster did it right enough. He's a menace where women are concerned.'

'Why? Have there been other incidents?'

'Not yet, no. But he hasn't been here that long.'

'Mrs Danbury, I think you ought to be careful what you say. What possible authority have you got for talking like this about a man?'

'The best in the world, Doctor. His own wife!'

It was sunset before Linda drove into the village of Stoke Dabenham and up to the big house that served as home and surgery for Doctor Cooper.

She parked her car in the yard and climbed the

wooden stairs to her flat in the stable block.

She went to the telephone, kicking off her shoes as she crossed the room, and dialled the surgery.

'Any messages, Mrs Perry?'

'I always put the messages on the desks, Doctor Ford.'

'Yes, thank you. And are there any?'

'No. Only for Doctor Cooper.'

'Right.'

Linda made a mental note. Always remember to report to headquarters before going off duty!

But I'm lucky, thought Linda. The flat was no more than two rooms with kitchen and bathroom, but it was pretty, with its old beams, whitewashed walls and cheerful cottage chintz.

And Doctor Cooper had asked her over to supper again. They were pleasant and useful these meals they were having together. John Cooper was a widower; and in his late sixties, Linda guessed. He'd been very kind so far and she was anxious to do the right things to please him.

She chose a plain navy dress and cheered it up with some fun beads. Maybe she'd risk more casual clothes later. She gave a final despairing spray at her hair – really, curls were pretty undignified! But curls were hers by nature. Then she set off across to the house, going in through the back door.

Elsie Peach was standing over the stove with her hat already on.

'Mrs Perry's gone, the telephone's switched through, the supper's on the hob, and the Doctor's late back from rounds again.'

'You pop off, Mrs Peach. I'll bring it to the table.'

'Are you sure it's no bother?'

Elsie picked up a bowl of fruit salad and carried it through to the dining room.

Linda followed with a basket of bread rolls.

'There's steak-and-kidney pie and the cream for the fruit is on the sideboard,' said Elsie.

'Sounds lovely.'

Linda had stopped in front of a photograph. It was of a young man much her own age.

'That's the Doctor's son.'

'I know.' Hadn't his father told her so the first evening? His voice warm with pride at his son's achievements in Medical School.

'He's a lovely young man.'

'I can see.'

'You'll like him.'

Peter Cooper regarded them from his frame. Don't disturb me, lovely young man, said Linda silently. I deserve a little peace. The door is locked, lovely young man. This property is off the market. The last tenant was a vandal and left the premises in great disorder.

'Good night then,' called Elsie, making for the door. 'It's very nice to have someone bright round the place again. The old partner got to be a right devil before he passed on, God rest him. 'Course everybody thought young Doctor Peter would join his father now he's qualified.'

'Perhaps he will yet, Elsie. I'm only here for six months you know.'

'Oh lovely!' Elsie trotted off.

Just keeping his seat warm, that's all, thought Linda; and she made a face at the photograph.

Left alone, Linda wandered into the lounge and towards an old mandolin propped in a dark corner. She'd spotted it before and admired its intricate mother-of-pearl decoration.

Lifting it down, she plucked at it gently, picking out an old melody.

She knew it was wrong played in this fashion but it

gave her pleasure to handle the rare instrument.

She sat down, crossed her legs and experimented. In her student days she'd played a rather mean guitar, and they'd all sung. What were the songs?

She'd just finished the second chorus of *Foggy Foggy Dew* when a round of applause greeted her from the door.

Linda turned guiltily, jolted back from old memories.

'You're musical, I see, Doctor Ford.' John Cooper stepped towards her. 'That is not, of course, the way to play it.'

'No, I know, I was just –'

He took the mandolin from her. 'Is that meant to be soup on the stove? Where's Mrs Peach?'

'I let her go. It's all right, I'll serve.'

'Excellent. And after coffee you can play me gems from the shows.'

Linda grinned sheepishly and made for the kitchen.

With his second helping of pie, Cooper began to talk shop, and Linda listened carefully to the useful background information he vouchsafed.

When Betty Danbury's name happened to come up, it was agreed, although she was John Cooper's patient, that Linda should continue to visit her if necessary, since she had two other cases in the vicinity.

'Mrs Danbury seems a rather – forthright character,' said Linda, carefully.

'Mm. Lost her husband at sea. Guards her children like a watchdog. Thought they'd have a man in the family again when Betty got a fellow, but the rascal scarpered and all they got was another mouth to feed. Betty didn't seem bothered – rather relieved in fact since she'd gone off the chap – but Mrs D. staves off all comers and waits for his unlikely return with the tenacity of Madam Butterfly!'

***

When Linda called again at Roseberry Cottage, Betty seemed quite well; and a fortnight went by, during which Linda alternated at the surgery in Stoke Dabenharn and the little outpost at Pretting which the doctors manned twice a week. She was getting to know her regulars now, was familiar with the voice of the local policeman, and of the matron of the Cottage Hospital; and she didn't need to call on Mrs Perry's help with the files quite so often.

Then one evening a telephone call announced an incident up at Mead Orchards. Betty Danbury had been found unconscious under a tree again – and Mr Foster had been hit on the head with an axe. Linda decided Foster's need could be the most urgent.

Mead Orchards straggled unevenly over nearly a mile of countryside and the apples, grown for cider, this year were in great abundance and hung ready for picking. At last Linda saw the house. There were apple trees up to its door and Linda, picking her way through half-eaten windfalls, disturbed clouds of dropsical wasps.

'Who are you?'

Linda started. The door had been flung open at her knock and a woman stood on the threshold staring with hostile eyes.

'I'm the doctor. I believe there's been a –'

'I rang Doctor Cooper.'

'I'm afraid he wasn't available. He –'

'Don't you come in here. I've had enough trouble from your sort!'

'Christine, for God's sake!'

A man's voice came from inside, and as the woman turned, Linda stepped into the hall, where she could see a man bending over the kitchen sink. He was holding a flannel to his forehead and blood was running between his fingers and dripping into a bowl. Linda went towards him.

'Don't you touch him!' The woman screamed.

Ignoring her, Linda sat the man in a chair, drew back his head and started to clean him up.

'I'm sorry, Doctor,' said Foster. 'Christine, now the doctor's here for heaven's sake let her fix me up.'

'Oh yes! I knew you'd like that! Just your cup of tea!'

'Will you please be quiet!' The man winced.

'It's not a deep cut,' said Linda, briskly. 'The head always bleeds prodigiously and you weren't helping matters stooping over and bathing it with hot water.'

'The blade didn't catch me. I dodged. It was just the haft. I don't know what the boy thought he was doing.'

'Well I do,' the woman interjected. 'Defending his sister – against a man like you!'

Foster sucked in an angry breath. 'She's talking nonsense.'

'I told Betty Danbury's mother – you stop your girl passing through my husband's land, because he can't resist anything in skirts and he'll be after her, sure as fate.'

'I've never even spoken to the girl!'

'Would her brother have come after you for nothing? Don't take me for a fool!'

'It's not true. I swear.' The denial was utterly weary.

'Hold still, Mr Foster,' said Linda, and hurried on quickly. 'Now then, I've stopped the bleeding. It's not bad enough to need stitches. I'll put you on a dressing and you must sit still for a while.'

'Thank you, Doctor.'

'Why should I put up with it? Why should I stay with him?' Mrs Foster was hugging her own thin body and rocking herself in agitation. 'Running after every bit of a girl he sets eyes on. You'll see for yourself if I go out of the room. But then you'll probably like that!'

Linda dressed the scalp wound in record time. Before

she left she gave Foster two tablets. 'Take one of these if the head's painful,' she said. 'And Mrs Foster might find the other helpful. She's had a shock, I think.'

That the woman was emotionally disturbed was obvious. But was there something in the story about Betty Danbury? Well, she'd soon know.

But she didn't. Betty was adamant that no one had assaulted her in any way, whilst her mother was equally positive that she was lying to protect Foster. But the fact remained that the girl had been found by her mother in the middle of the orchard, collapsed under a tree, and again there were angry red marks to be seen.

Linda examined them closely and frowned.

On her way out she came across the boy Dick and took the chance to discourage him from further violence – even to avenge his sister's honour.

'After all,' she pointed out, 'you may have hit the wrong man.'

'Ma said he did it,' said Dick Danbury simply. 'And my sister Betty's a good girl.'

'And she says he *didn't*, doesn't she?'

The boy gave a defeated grunt, stuck his hands in his pockets and made off towards his ferret hutch.

During the next two weeks Linda drove past the Orchards several times on her way to see patients. There were many people in them now, for the apples were being picked. Lorryloads of the rosy fruit nosed their way from the fields to the presses and by the end of the fortnight the trees were stripped of their harvest.

Linda heard no more of the Danburys until Betty brought the baby into surgery with a slight tummy upset. As she was going, Linda asked her whether she'd had any more fainting fits.

'No I haven't, Doctor. And wasn't Ma silly? But it's all blown over now. Mr Foster sent to ask whether he could give me a basket of Cox's as a sort of peace-offering – and Ma's said yes. So everything's all right.'

'Good. I'm finished now. If you hang on I'll give you a lift back. I have to go out that way.'

'Oh thanks. It'll be an hour before the bus comes.'

When they were driving by Mead Orchards, Betty looked up sideways at Linda.

'It would save time if you put me down here,' she said.

They pulled up. It was true. There was Roseberry Cottage in sight through the trees.

Linda grinned. 'Right. But I'll walk you across. I'll never be able to face your mother again otherwise!'

Together they crossed the orchard, discussing matters concerning the baby, which Betty carried tenderly, its downy head pressed to her cheek.

At the gate they parted. But as Linda turned back she caught sight of a figure hovering behind a tree. It was Mrs Foster, and her face was a mask of venom.

As Betty went indoors, the woman turned away and walked off. Linda was glad the girl had not seen the blatant malice in the woman's eyes.

It was only a matter of hours before Linda was once more hurrying towards Roseberry Cottage. She did not need to knock on the door, Mrs Danbury ran down the path to meet her.

'He's poisoned her! Poisoned her!' She hustled Linda inside, pounded upstairs to the bedroom and flung out a dramatic finger. 'Look what he's done!'

Betty was certainly in a bad way. She was flushed and breathless and had vomited several times.

'What happened?' asked Linda, feeling for the girl's pulse.

'I just ate one of the apples,' panted Betty, 'and I came over queer.'

'It's because she won't have nothing to do with him!' cried Mrs Danbury.

'Oh Ma!' Betty's eyes filled with tears.

'Now calm down, Mrs Danbury,' said Linda sharply. 'There are several other possibilities. It's far more likely Betty has some sort of allergy. That apples disagree with her.'

'Oh no they don't,' argued Mrs Danbury. 'She's always eaten them before.'

Linda looked at Betty, who nodded.

'I've always liked them very much,' she admitted.

'We've never had this palaver before. Those apples have been tampered with.'

'Where are they now?' asked Linda.

'Gone back where they come from. My Dicker threw the lot back into Foster's yard.'

That's helpful, thought Linda.

She made Betty comfortable and took various specimens for testing; then made her escape from Mrs Danbury – with a parting warning to that lady to keep Betty undisturbed.

Back in her consulting room, Linda settled down to write some letters. There was a tap on the door, and Mrs Perry entered with a cup of tea.

'Would you like a sandwich, Doctor? It's getting on for evening surgery and you've had no break.'

Linda smiled gratefully.

'No thanks I'm nearly through then I'll slip back to the flat.'

'There's a very heavy surgery. You do know?'

'Yes, Mrs Perry.' Linda matched the impersonal tone. 'Would you send off these specimens from Betty Danbury for analysis, please.'

Linda watched her go, then began to pen a note to her parents. They'd made sacrifices to put her through Medical School and she tried to send frequent field messages back to the small, old-fashioned dairy in the East

End of London, where her career was being so anxiously followed.

'... Mrs Perry is playing it very cool,' she wrote, 'but she knows her job. I think it may be harder to win her confidence than Doctor Cooper's! He seems to like me, but his brows beetle rather ominously. If I do something really stupid (which mercifully I haven't yet) I fear his wrath could be a bit flattening. But right now I know I can go to him for advice when I need it – and that's a comfort.'

Later, when her last patient had departed – and there *had* been a vast queue, Mrs Perry was right of course – Linda found herself seeking out Doctor Cooper for some of that advice. They went through to the lounge and sank into easy chairs, and he passed her a glass of sherry as she described Betty Danbury's condition.

'Have there been any similar cases in the area, Doctor Cooper?' queried Linda.

'You're thinking of a toxic spray.'

'It crossed my mind.'

'Not that I've heard of. But it's a possibility. Have you got any of the apples?'

'No. They were thrown away.'

'That's helpful.'

Linda smiled.

'You shouldn't have allowed that, Doctor Ford.'

The smile slipped sideways and off.

'Check with Foster what he doped his apples with this year.'

Linda nodded. She'd planned to do just that.

'Could be something new – or used too strong in quantity.'

'Mrs Danbury's convinced it was done on purpose,' said Linda.

'What's she been reading, *Snow White and the Seven Dwarfs*?'

'She's serious. And Foster's been cast as the wicked witch, which is hard, since he seems to have a home-grown one of his own.'

'Doctor Ford –'

'I'm sorry, but I never saw such a fiendishly jealous woman. The man's life must be a misery.'

'He hasn't complained, Doctor, and it is not our business to make judgements.'

Linda took the rebuke. It was true. One had to remain objective.

The next morning, Linda telephoned to Foster and he offered to look out the remains of the pesticide he'd used on his trees. He was very concerned about Betty's illness and worried at the thought of any chemical he'd used being the cause. Linda passed this fact on to Mrs Danbury in an attempt to mollify her, for Betty was still quite ill.

Patiently, Linda put it to her that although there could have been a dangerous liquid sprayed on the apples it must have been by accident.

'It was no accident,' maintained Mrs Danbury. 'Nobody sends poisoned apples to someone by accident. He's got it in for her that's clear. But just let him wait till Betty's man comes back!'

Linda attended to Betty without another word. Detachment. That's what Doctor Cooper had recommended.

But Betty looked wretched and it wasn't only because she wasn't well.

As she left the house, Linda was aware of Betty's brother emerging from the landing and trailing her downstairs.On the path to the gate he finally stepped in front of her, took a deep breath and blurted out a statement that made Linda grab him by the shoulder and drag him back indoors to his mother.

'Mrs Danbury! Listen to this, please! Young man, repeat what you just told me.'

Dick Danbury avoided his mother's eye but he obeyed the command.

'They weren't poisoned, Ma. I ate a couple of them before Betty did.'

It must be an allergy. Linda was now convinced. She drove straight to Foster's. At least it would put his mind at rest to know there was nothing wrong with the apples.

It did; and his relief was considerable – and more significant than Linda had realised.

'Thank God!' he said. 'I thought – I wondered whether –'

His eyes went to his wife, who was sitting in the garden with her back turned to them.

'I'll still take a sample of that pesticide, Mr Foster.'

'I'll get it – but it's only one in common use.'

The sound of their voices had reached Mrs Foster, and as her husband went off towards an outbuilding, she rose and came straight to Linda.

'You're here again, are you?'

'Your husband's helping me with an enquiry.'

I sound like a policeman, thought Linda, but what did one say to those accusing eyes.

'Did you know my husband sent that girl a basket of apples?'

Did she not.

'Presents now, you see? He'll have his way yet, you see. She might as well have given in when he tried it on in the orchard!'

'Mrs Foster, how can I persuade you you're wrong. Listen, your husband did send Betty some apples – and she ate one and is still ill from it. The girl's recently had a baby. That can be quite an upheaval to the system, do you understand? I think she may have developed an apple-allergy. There was nothing wrong with that fruit yet she's been violently sick. And that's why, I think, she was overcome in the orchard. She wasn't attacked or assaulted. She was alone! It was the apples themselves. She had a dramatic physical reaction to them.'

'It won't wash you know.'

'Mrs Foster, I assure you it's absolutely possible. And tests will prove –'

'I'll be surprised if they do. You've got a short memory, haven't you? You went across that orchard yourself with that girl. She didn't get "overcome" that time did she? I know she didn't. I saw you both.'

It was a fact. Linda suddenly remembered. But there was something ...

Foster was coming towards them. His wife at once whirled round on him and her voice began climbing into hysteria. Recriminations and abuse flowed in a wild tirade.

Foster's face was white and drawn. 'Will you go, Doctor, I can manage her better alone.'

'Would you like me to –'

'Please. It's all right.'

Mrs Foster's scene reached its climax. 'I'm going! I'm going! I don't have to go on living with a man like you! I'm leaving!' She rushed into the house.

'She'll change her mind,' said Foster, and followed her.

But a few days later Linda heard from Elsie Peach, who was a better source of local information than the *Gazette*, that Mrs Foster had indeed departed, but not before she had broadcast her reasons, and stirred up quite a bit of local feeling against Foster.

'Have they got a sex maniac loose up there?' asked John Cooper quizzically.

'I hope not,' said Linda earnestly, 'but how do you tell?'

'You get better at it as the years go by – but there's always the surprise that confounds you.'

He was handing Linda the name of the Consultant

who would decide whether to test Betty for an allergy.

'Thank you for this,' she said. 'Though I'm not sure whether it's worth her seeing him now.'

'What about the analysis you had done?'

'Negative. I must confess, both the toxic spray and anaphylaxis theories seem knocked on the head.'

'Very thwarting.'

'Yet I had such a *feeling* –' she stopped.

She felt he'd disapprove of that line of thought.

Instead he said, 'Intuition can be very valuable, my dear. Don't discount it.'

Encouraged, Linda went on, half to herself. 'It's exasperating. Four times that girl came in close contact with apples. Three of those times she was seriously upset. Once she ate one and was ill; straightforward enough. Twice she was found unconscious under the apple trees in the middle of the orchard. But why didn't she faint when I was with her?'

'Tiresome of her.'

With an effort Linda dismissed the puzzle from her mind, and turned her attention to a case history about which John Cooper was giving her some information.

'You'll see,' he was saying, 'it has occurred to three separate members of this particular family with identical symptoms. Whichever name I had picked – if, for instance, I'd picked –'

'Picked!' Linda interrupted him. 'That's it! Picked! I'm sorry, Doctor Cooper, I didn't mean to make you jump. But it's the answer. When Betty and I went through that orchard it was after it had been picked. There were only a few windfalls about – not enough to affect her. Ha!

'Where's that name? We'll make an appointment for Betty to see the Consultant immediately! I was right! Right!'

'I hope the jubilation isn't because it's a rare occurrence,' remarked Cooper.

Betty's tests proved positive, but in a week she had fully recovered from her attack, and now knew to avoid the troublesome fruit for the time being. A course of immunisation injections was suggested, if the reaction did not subside of its own accord.

It was only a minor victory but Linda's self-confidence got a little boost. She believed in herself as a doctor but she knew it would take time before she inspired the trust she recognised in the faces of John Cooper's patients. But when Mrs Danbury stopped her in the street and said awkwardly: 'I apologised to that Foster. I thought you'd like to know, Doctor' Linda was touched.

She saw Betty herself two weeks later, making her way down the lane with a load of shopping, and gave her a lift to the orchard gate. As they drew up, Foster was stepping through it. He remained holding it open for Betty.

'It's safe right now,' said Betty. 'I mean – while there's no apples.'

'Safe till next summer then,' he said.

They stood for a moment looking at each other. Linda realised that they were meeting for the first time – these two whose lives had been so entwined by circumstance.

Then they both smiled – very tentatively.

He took the shopping bag and, with a distance of four feet between them, they walked across the orchard. Slowly. Not speaking. There was no hurry.

The radio contact signalled to Linda.

'Mrs Jameson phoned, Doctor Ford. Can you go to Weatherlands.'

'The baby?'

'Yes. It's Upchurch Green and you go by Dampton Mill and –'

'I know, Mrs Perry. It's that lovely National Trust property isn't it?'

'That's right. You should look over its gardens some time, Doctor.' The voice was friendly now. That very morning, Linda and Mrs Perry had discovered a mutual attachment to African Violets. Linda's uncle had grown them in his bedroom and Mrs Perry had a whole greenhouse devoted to them and promised Linda one or two for her flat. It was like finding the key to a locked door.

The setting sun was reflected in the millstream by the time Linda finally left Weatherlands.

I could put down a root or two myself, she thought later, sitting on a rug by the fire and gazing at her reflection in a copper jug on the hearth. But I'd better not. This is the clever young Doctor Peter's scene, when he chooses to take the stage.

She reached for a magazine and an apple. An apple! Ye Gods! She sank her teeth into it recklessly.

CHAPTER TWO

OCCUPATIONAL HAZARD

Linda knocked a third time on the weathered cottage door. Charming people! she thought, calling urgently for the doctor then calmly going out. Yet the voice had sounded anxious enough on the phone, too agitated in fact to give her proper details. Linda hoped this wasn't going to be the habit of many of her new patients.

She raised her hand to give the door another buffet. There was a movement at an upstairs window. Linda stepped back and looked up. The small white face of a young boy stared down at her with frightened eyes, then quickly withdrew.

So someone was inside. Linda felt irritated, then alarmed. 'An accident!' the voice had said. She pushed against the door, and as she did so, saw the rusted hinges and yellow spider-eggs. It couldn't have been opened in years! Then she remembered something Doctor Cooper had said when she'd first joined his practice. 'In some of the remoter parts round here they never use the front door. You go round to the back.'

Linda started down the side of the house, picking her way along a brick path and between an outcrop of sheds. Drips from a recent shower spattered her from corrugated roofs and the yard at the back of the house looked like Flanders Field.

Beyond the property stretched green fields, decorated with a vast moving pattern of white hens and dotted with orderly nesting-houses. A dog saw Linda and began to bark. At once a woman appeared from an outbuilding, carrying a bucket. She put it down and hurried across.

'Are you the doctor?'

Linda nodded.

The woman led the way into the house, slipping off her heavy shoes in the doorway. Probably a pretty woman when she smiled, Linda thought, but now she was drawn and distracted. Too distracted to give Linda the usual glance of appraisal which, as the new young woman doctor in the district, she had come to expect.

They went into a small sitting-room, where a man was lying back in an armchair, his large frame covered with a blanket. His shoulder was thickly swathed with sheeting.

'I made him as comfortable as I could,' said the woman, going straight to his side and taking his hand.

'What happened?'

'An accident with the gun. He was climbing over a stile and he slipped. The gun went off by accident.'

The woman spoke with a faint accent that Linda could not place. The man just nodded.

'You should have told me this,' said Linda, unwrapping the shoulder. 'Are you on the telephone?'

'It's not bad enough for hospital,' said the man, reading her thoughts.

'We'll see,' said Linda, using the cheerful but firm voice that she felt to be suitable for a General Practitioner. In hospital the patients were mostly overawed and respectful, cowed by their surroundings, and Linda missed this bulwark behind her. As a mere locum, young, pretty and temporary, she was anxious to win respect for her authority.

But the wound was not as serious as it might have been.

'You're lucky. Very lucky, Mr Tomkins. Another couple of inches and the bullet would have been into your lung.'

As it was, it had passed straight through the soft flesh under his arm, just missing the shoulder blade.

Linda brought dressings from her car and cleaned and bandaged the man's shoulder.

'How did it come to happen?'

'It was the jolt it got. Me falling on it, like.'

'How was it that you fell?'

'My boot slipped.'

'He carries it over his shoulder like this, you see?' Mrs Tomkins was demonstrating. 'And as he fell off the stile it hit against the fence and made the trigger go off.'

'Yes. Just like that,' the man added.

Their eyes were fixed guardedly on Linda's reactions.

'It's easy to slip with all this mud,' the woman went on quickly, 'and where the stile leads into the meadow it's very bad. It is where the cows stand, you see, and –'

'Is that the gun?' Linda asked, pointing to the corner of the room. 'What sort is it?'

'Point two-two – for shootin' vermin.'

Linda finished dealing with the wound. 'We must get him to his bed.'

'Yes, Doctor,' said Mrs Tomkins. 'I'll go up and make ready.' And she hurried away.

'I'll be in tomorrow to see how you are, Mr Tomkins.'

'I'll be all right.'

'You don't know what a narrow escape you had. You'd better save that bullet for a souvenir, if you can find it.'

'That'll be easy enough.'

'Easy? What out in a field?'

'Oh. Oh no – I was forgetting –' Linda looked at him curiously and he avoided her eye.

Linda closed her bag and carried it out into the hall. She felt vaguely troubled. It was shadowy, and it gave her a start as she became aware of a figure crouched back under the stairs. It was the boy whose face she'd seen at the window. He was about thirteen years old and Linda had never seen a youngster look so stricken. From his resemblance to the man in the sitting-room she guessed it was his son.

'Don't worry, lad,' she said. 'He's going to be quite all right.'

'I wish he were *dead*!' The boy hissed out the words then ran off down the passage.

Linda stared after him, completely taken aback.

There was a step on the stairs and Mrs Tomkins came down.

'I've got everything ready,' she said and passed into the sitting room without a glance down the passage although Linda could have sworn she had heard the boy's words.

Together the two women assisted the heavy man up to the bedroom, removed his clothes and got him settled. For a man who had taken a severe tumble in the mud, there was remarkably little on his clothes, Linda reflected. In fact, there was *too* little. *Far too little*.

Linda was still pondering on this point as she climbed into her car. As she switched on the engine a head poked through the window beside her.

'Excuse me, my dear. You're the new doctor, aren't you? You'll give an old lady a lift down the village won't you, my love?'

'Of course.' Linda opened the door and a wiry, nut-brown little woman got in beside her, clutching a bedraggled shopping-bag to her bosom.

'Saw you arrive, I did. I give hand with the chicken

down by. They're in trouble this time, aren't they?'

'Mr Tomkins? Well, it could have been worse.' Linda put the engine into top and speeded up. She had a feeling the woman was set on extracting from her a few juicy titbits to gossip over. But instead she spread her own rich banquet.

'Dutch, she is. Strangers always bring trouble. Got himself to blame, right enough. Marrying a foreigner like that. Running up to London like that and bringing back a girl nobody ever clapped eyes on before. His own fault, what's happened.'

The woman suddenly craned her neck to look back down the road.

'There's two of old Abel's sheep loose,' she said, with satisfaction. 'Where was I? Oh yes, George Tomkins brought it on himself. Stands to reason a girl like that – not belonging in these parts – she doesn't fit in. Nor her son neither. Soft in the head the lad is. Didn't I see him myself? Cryin' his eyes out down by the pond when he finds the kittens Abel drowned. And him all of thirteen. And comes home from school most days with a bruise that his father'll give him one to match for getting! Boy's soft and everybody knows it. That's what comes of marrying foreigners. And George Tomkins never got shot falling over a stile, I warrant!'

Linda brought the car to a halt in the village street and her passenger got out.

'This'll do fine, my dear, and thank you. I do hope you'll be happy in Stoke Dabenham, Miss – er, Doctor Ford, living up there with Doctor Cooper. Just the two of you.'

'I have a flat in the stable block, as a matter of fact!'

Linda could have kicked herself for rising to the bait.

'My dear life, that must be cosy. Bye bye then. I'll be in surgery as usual on Tuesday with my leg.'

It is cosy, thought Linda, as she soaked in a warm bath.

Linda had been angry at the woman's spiteful attack on the Tomkins, but the scented water and comforting steam were mellowing her mood. Nevertheless there was something amiss there. She knew it and felt a sense of foreboding. Tomorrow! she said to herself firmly, and climbed out of the bath to attend to the serious business of dressing.

When Linda got over to the big house Doctor Cooper was not yet back, but there was a fire in the lounge and Linda strolled in and settled in an armchair by it, picking up a newspaper. 'Shots Fired Across Border. Israelis Claim –' She laid the paper down. Shots fired. That gun up at the Tomkins.

That wasn't muddy either. And *how* was it Mrs Tomkins had said it happened? Linda went into the hall and took a walking stick from the stand. Back in the lounge she climbed on a chair and jumped off, letting the stick fall in the way described by the Tomkins. It didn't seem to work. She climbed back on to the chair, hung the walking stick on her shoulder and was about to launch herself into space again.

'What in the world are you doing, Doctor?'

Linda regained her balance, stepped down from the chair and apologised to Doctor Cooper, who stood in the doorway staring at her in astonishment.

'I didn't hear you come in.'

'Obviously!' The voice came from behind the older man, where, to her horror, Linda saw a second figure and recognised instantly who it was.

'I thought you were out on a call,' said Linda.

'No, I went to the station to pick up my son. If you'll come down off the furniture I'll introduce you.'

Linda climbed down, feeling a complete idiot. And the mocking twinkle in the eye of the young man did little to help matters.

It took Linda what felt like four hours to pull on her

shoes, then she straightened her shoulders and held out her hand.

'How do you do,' she said.

'The flying doctor, I presume,' said the young man.

Linda laughed. She had no alternative.

'Peter is down on a brief visit. No warning. Usual pattern! You two get to know each other, I'll rustle up some extras from the kitchen.'

Doctor Cooper left the room, and Linda found herself under the scrutiny of his son. It was a challenging, appraising regard.

All right, thought Linda, so you're worried that your father has a fool for a locum. Well, you are quite mistaken, sonny boy.

'Your father has told me so much about you,' said Linda. It wasn't strictly true, but it scored her a point in the little duel they were engaged in.

'And it's all true,' said Peter, cheerfully.

But his ears went pink, and Linda suddenly liked him better.

He poured them both a sherry.

'Were you up on the chair for any particular reason? Mouse? Flood warning?'

'I must have looked ridiculous, but there was a serious purpose. There was an accident today – with a gun. I was trying to see how it could possibly have happened – and I don't think it could have. Not like they said.'

'Tell us about it at supper,' said Doctor Cooper, entering on her words. 'And I'll be very much obliged if you'll stay down off the furniture. I'm too tired to set any broken bones this evening.'

When they'd drunk their soup, Cooper gave her his permission to talk. At once Linda told him about the incident at the Tomkins.

'– and there was no mud either on his clothes and the

rifle and I'm sure it could never have happened the way she said. In fact, I'm as certain as I'm sitting here that Mrs Tomkins was lying!' Linda flung down her spoon heatedly.

'More than likely, my dear. More than likely,' said Cooper equably. 'If you were as familiar with the intrigues and deceits of the female sex as I am, you wouldn't find it so surprising.'

'But –'

'Challenge her, Doctor Ford, challenge her. Tell her you don't believe a word of her pack of nonsense.'

'She *seemed* nice enough,' said Linda.

'They all do. They all do.' Cooper cut himself more pie.

'But her story was definitely untrue.'

'Catch her out, my dear. Go ahead. Have no mercy.'

'My word, father, we're in a very belligerent mood,' said Peter.

'Do you wonder. Six miles out to see Mrs Mandeville, only to have her clasp my hand and whisper the time for an assignation.'

'Oh dear.'

Linda knew Mrs Mandeville was a newcomer to the district and had definite designs on Cooper, luring him to her house on any pretext. So far the doctor had nimbly avoided her wiles.

'It's a battle of wits,' said Cooper cheerfully, 'but I have a plan to confound the woman. I propose to turn up at the "wrong" time – in fact when her husband is home, which will, I hope, both infuriate her and embarrass her, since there is nothing wrong with her whatsoever.'

'What a devilish plot,' said Linda, laughing.

''Tis rather. Have some more salad.'

'You've yet to know my father,' said Peter. 'Don't be fooled by that old-world, disarming bedside manner.'

'Nothing wrong with a bit of charm, my boy, to help

the medicine go down.'

'I'll remember that,' said Peter, and turned to refill Linda's wine glass with a heart-stopping smile.

A chip off the old block all right, thought Linda. A good thing I'm older and wiser than I was or ...

'To more serious matters,' said Peter, leaning towards her earnestly. 'Tell us the intimate details of your personal life.'

'Certainly not,' laughed Linda. 'They're not suitable for your innocent ears.'

'I might have guessed. I should think you've caused a bit of a stir down here in Sleepy Hollow.'

'Of course. Wild parties. The lads of the village battering my door down –'

'And who could blame them, indeed.'

Under his searching eye, Linda was lost for words and began concentrating on her plate.

She was usually a fair match for this kind of banter. She felt cross with herself for finding his physical nearness attractive and distracting. She must keep her cool with this self-assured gentleman.

'You didn't bring Susan down this time then, Peter,' said Doctor Cooper.

'No, she'd got her head down in work. Needs to catch up a bit.'

So he has a girlfriend, thought Linda. That's all right then. Yes. Good. Splendid.

'Has Susan fallen seriously behind?' asked the older doctor.

'Don't think so. Not sure really. Haven't seen much of her lately.'

So there wasn't a girlfriend. Ah.

'I'm a couple of ladies behind, am I,' observed John Cooper.

'Yes,' said Peter. And they all laughed.

When Linda called at the Tomkins next day, the man

looked better and said his wound was easing. The boy was nowhere in sight.

After medical matters were dealt with she took a deep breath and went into the attack.

'I don't believe what you said about the shooting, you know.'

The husband and wife exchanged looks and Linda felt the atmosphere grow tense.

'It's true, I tell you –' the man began to bluster.

'Very well,' said Linda. 'Stick to it if you like but you don't convince me and I don't think the police will accept it.'

There was panic in their eyes as they looked at her.

Linda went towards the door.

'George!' pleaded Mrs Tomkins.

'All right,' said the man reluctantly. 'Tell her.'

'Wait! Doctor Ford! We'll tell you the truth. Please listen.'

With difficulty she began. 'Then you will understand why we did not wish it known. It is all my fault. I – I – there was another man. A foolish affair that brought me only pain. My husband found out at last and there was a great quarrel. He threatened with a gun. There was a struggle. Somehow – I don't know how it happened – my lover got hold of it. He did not mean to shoot, but it went off.'

Mrs Tomkins was turned away from Linda with her eyes cast down.'Now it is all over. My husband says he will forgive me. My – my friend is leaving the country. Please do not tell the police. Let him go! Let it all be forgotten!'

Mr Tomkins nodded agreement.

'I doubt whether you can keep it quiet, you know,' said Linda, thinking of the gossiping woman to whom she'd given a lift.

If there were many more like her in this harsh and

isolated little community, it would soon get round.

'Doctor, it is a chance to start again. And now if there is more trouble –' She hid her face in her hands.

Linda was perplexed.

That the woman was genuinely distressed she had no doubt, but nonetheless she had the feeling that she was not at the bottom of the matter. Linda pressed the woman's thin shoulder and she drew herself together.

'I'll be in again.' Linda made her escape through the back door.

It was no good. Mrs Tomkins just wasn't the type. Yet was there a type? People were plunging into unsuitable relationships every minute of the day.

Linda thought of her own unhappy experience – and noted with relief that the stab of pain was blunter. No, there wasn't a type; it happened to anybody.

But there had been something too secure and long-committed in the way the Tomkins had taken hands on the occasion of her first visit.

As Linda walked to her car she caught sight of the boy perched in the low branches of an old tree, hugging the dog to his chest.

As she looked towards him, he cowered back muttering into the dog's ear and watching her with wary eyes. She knew if she took a step in his direction he would be off across the windswept fields. She shivered and hurried to climb into the shelter of the car.

Linda took surgery at the village of Pretting that evening. The gas fire was giving out less heat than usual and seemed to have digestive trouble, but there were only two patients. One was an old man with a cough who eyed Linda suspiciously, but the other was a shy woman with piles, who said she was glad it was Linda taking surgery. This was cheering and Linda sped back to Stoke Dabenham humming to the radio.

She decided to write home that night. It was always a good idea to write to her parents when she was feeling confident. Their support had been so important to her, and she liked them to feel it had paid off.

But later the thought of the mystery of the Tomkins came nagging back and she felt herself floundering again.

'You're a doctor, not a detective,' Cooper reminded her when she brought the matter up again while the three doctors were taking coffee together.

'But one must *care*!' said Linda. 'A splint, a few pills, a bottle of medicine – that's not the sum total of it!'

'My dear girl –'

'There's something terribly wrong up at that chicken farm. That boy! If ever I saw a disturbed child, it's him! Why? There's a man with a wound in his shoulder, but the pain I see in his eyes is nothing to do with that. There's deeper trouble and I want to deal with it.'

'They've not called you for that though,' said Peter.

'Why do I have to wait till someone breaks down, till some tragedy occurs perhaps? When you see a person in stress surely you should take action!'

Cooper sat back in his chair and regarded her earnest face.

'But what action can you possibly take?' said Peter.

'I don't know! I don't know!'

'That's just it.' Cooper sighed. 'Use your eyes and use your ears,' he said, 'and keep cool.'

'But –'

'The last thing your patients need is your emotional involvement. Believe me!' said Peter. And his father nodded.

Linda accepted they were right.

But it didn't make her feel easier. She couldn't just "switch off" her concern.

The telephone rang. Linda recognised the sultry voice of the predatory Mrs Mandeville asking for Doctor Cooper.

'Shall I say you're out?' whispered Linda helpfully.

'Certainly not,' said Cooper, taking the instrument readily.

'Now Mrs Mandeville, what seems to be the trouble this time?' He winked at Linda and began to handle the delicate situation with obvious enjoyment.

Peter walked Linda over to her flat.

'I envy your father his experience,' said Linda. 'I'm full of uncertainties.'

'Well, let's face it, you've not been at it for long –'

'I spent a year in hospital in the East End of London!'

'Ah, but you don't know country ways. I was brought up here and I know the people are different. They'll only tell you what they want you to know. They won't want you to go nosing about.'

'That's just too bad! I'll certainly go nosing about – as you put it – if I get a bad scent.'

'Look, take my advice, you'll be better devoting your time to curing the sick than getting involved in some imagined psychological problems of the locals. And as for the Tomkins scene – forget it. Goodnight, Linda.'

And he actually patted her hand before striding off.

Linda watched him go with indignation building. Really! Dutch Uncle time! And he's hardly been qualified any longer than me! What's more, not been in General Practice at all yet. Saucy monkey!

She marched up her stairs and flung herself into an armchair. So! She'd sort out all that advice and accept what seemed reasonable. But as for forgetting the Tomkins problem – well she couldn't, and that was that.

That the boy was the key to the situation Linda had no doubt, and she resolved to find some means of tackling him. But it wasn't necessary. Two days later she came upon him outside the village shop. There was a knot of boys at the door and two figures threshing on the ground in violent battle. Linda drew her car into the kerb and ran towards the scene, pushing aside the passive onlookers and seizing hold of the attacker, she dragged him off. It was young Tomkins. His eyes were wild and his fists were red with blood from the other boy's nose which was streaming. Released, the victim quickly made off, leaving a trail of red stains down the road, and followed by his friends.

Linda shook the Tomkins boy. 'What do you think you are *doing*!'

'He called her a name! He called her a rotten name!' The boy was sobbing hysterically.

'Who?'

'Mum. My mother.'

'Get in the car.'

He sat next to her with tears pouring down his face as she drove quickly out of the village. Then she stopped and gave him a handkerchief to clean himself up.

How much did the boy know, she wondered.

'They're all talking about her. Whole village is talking about her. Saying she got a –' He searched for the words they'd used. It came out in a whisper, 'Fancy man.'

He didn't say more, but it was obvious the villagers had spared the child no details of what the words implied.

'It's not true!' he wept.

'Son, listen to me.' On impulse, Linda made her decision. 'Your parents have been through a bit of trouble and it's nobody's business but theirs.'

'What are you saying?' He was utterly bewildered.

'There was an argument and a struggle with the gun, and accidentally it went off –'

'Who told you this?'

'Your parents. But it's all over now. The important thing is that they love one another and want to make a new start and –'

'But it's lies you're telling. There was never any trouble between my mother and dad. It was *me* who shot at Dad! Not any "fancy man".'

'You!'

So this was what they had been trying to hide.

'Going for me and going for me. Telling me I'm soft and making fun of me. 'Cos I don't take after him or grandad who were a champion boxer in the county. Always going on 'cos I was no fighter. And that morning he threw away some flints I'd found. Said collecting stones was babyish. But they were special, see, I was taking them to the museum and he'd thrown them away! I was so mad I started crying, then he hit me and I grabbed hold of the gun and fired at him! But I missed. I only got his shoulder!' His bitterness was ugly and disturbing.

'Come home with me and have some tea.'

He sat silent and pale as they drove to the stable block, where Linda sat him down to buttered toast and jam, and told him to read a book till he felt better.

'I've a couple of things to pick up in surgery, then I'll take you home.'

Linda spotted Doctor Cooper in his garden, cutting back shrubs.

'Doctor Cooper!' She ran towards him.

'Japonica,' he said. 'Drastically overgrown. Needs major surgery.'

He performed the operation with enthusiasm.

'Doctor Cooper, I've got to the facts at last!'

'Thank heavens for that.'

Linda told him the boy's story, and Cooper looked thoughtful.

'I don't care what you advise, Doctor Cooper,' said Linda recklessly. 'I intend to say a word or two to Mr Tomkins! Bullying the boy into such a state! Just because the child doesn't happen to be a roughneck like some of those others! His own son! He can't have any feelings for him at all!'

'I'm not so sure.'

'Well I am! He's nothing but an arrogant man with an oversized pride.'

'Quite. And have you thought what it has cost that proud man to let that made-up story of his wife's infidelity be bandied round the district? You say he doesn't love the boy? I wonder. Think hard about those "words" you're going to have with him, Doctor Ford.'

Linda turned away in silence and went to fetch a sterile container she needed for old Mrs Ilsing's blood sample. She took her time, to give the boy a chance to collect himself. If he was still overwrought she might give him a mild sedative. But when she got back he seemed calmer although he had eaten very little. She sat down by the fire opposite him.

'What's your name?'

'Dave.'

'Listen, Dave, I believe what you say. That the tale is a lie. It didn't ring true when she told it to me. But it was *she herself* who told me, Dave, and your father didn't deny it. Why do you suppose they did that?'

'It wasn't right.'

'I know. But why did they make it up? Why didn't they say what really happened?'

'I don't know.'

'But what if they *had*? What if they'd told the truth?'

'I s'pose I'd have got in trouble.'

'You certainly would. And do you understand, Dave, that story that got about – it must have made your father feel very ashamed. I don't suppose he's been into the village much since.'

'No, he hasn't.' The boy frowned.

'And he did it for *you*, Dave. To shield you.'

The boy's face grew hard.

'I know he's made you unhappy, but – perhaps – perhaps he was afraid for you. The world's a tough place. He wanted you to hold your own.'

'I can't fight.'

'You were doing all right today!'

'I never done it afore. I made 'is nose bleed!'

He suddenly giggled.

'You know, I've a feeling, Dave, that things might be different between you and your father from now on. I feel sure he could never have known how much he was upsetting you. Won't you give him a chance? It's a big thing he's done for your sake, Dave, and he won't live it down in a hurry.'

There was no reply, but Linda looked into his face, from which the tension was now gone, and she felt hopeful.

'I better get home, please, Miss. My dad'll –' He paused thoughtfully, 'be worried.'

As they drove home to the farm, Linda could feel the boy's spirits rising.

'Super car! I like M.G.s. Even old ones.'

He looked a little surprised when they arrived and she got out.

'Are you coming in?'

'Yes. I want a word with your father.'

'Oh.' But he looked at her trustingly.

Linda hoped fervently that she would find the right things to say. She was grateful for Doctor Cooper's warning. She had been all set to blunder in with all guns blazing, and a lot of good that would have done everyone! Control. Composing her manner into one of serious but calm concern she went into the sitting room;

and was thrown completely off balance by Tomkins's immediate attack.

'What have you brought him home for? What's the boy been doing now?' he shouted.

'Fighting!' Linda shouted back, 'and, unlike you, I wouldn't think it anything to be proud of –'

'Fighting!' Tomkins jaw dropped.

'Except that in this case he was provoked beyond reasonable limits.'

'*Fighting?*'

'Yes! Those village boys, who you so much want him to be like, they greatly enjoyed jeering at his parents.'

Linda became aware of Mrs Tomkins standing rigidly in the doorway.

'And he went for them?'

'Very much so, Mr Tomkins. You've misjudged him very badly. So he doesn't go throwing his weight about and he's got a gentle nature, but he's got courage enough when it's really necessary.'

'He never showed it before.'

'What if he didn't? What good did it do the child to torment him until he was crazy enough to try to kill you!'

'Oh George!' The woman clung to him. 'She knows!'

'Can you imagine how desperate your son must have been to do such a thing?'

Tomkins's face whitened and he groped for his wife's hand as if lost. 'I never meant to drive him so far,' he whispered. 'I swear it. But he were laughing-stock of village, and that's a fact. I couldn't bear my friends all calling him soft. They pitied me.'

'Your *friends*, Mr Tomkins? If I were you I'd take a closer look at some of them. I think you might find that the ones who "pitied" you so much were quite ready to revel in the bit of scandal about your marriage!'

Mrs Tomkins looked at her husband intently. There

were years of local persecution etched in her face.

'We're cut off in this valley, you know, and they're a hard lot hereabout,' he admitted gruffly. 'Narrow too, I suppose, some of them.'

'And they're no yardstick to measure your son by, Mr Tomkins!' declared Linda.

Later that night, returning from a minor emergency, Linda was waylaid by John Cooper and invited in for a farewell drink with his son. Linda accepted with alacrity and took the opportunity to recount the news of the Tomkins, not without some pride, and leaving out the part where she'd shouted her head off.

'Mind you,' she finished, 'Tomkins was probably more impressed in the end by the fact that his son had bloodied his school-friend's nose than by my words of wisdom.'

'Very likely,' said Peter, aggravatingly.

'But I do think the situation is under control now.'

'That's as it should be,' said the older doctor, downing his Scotch. 'Let nothing you dismay. Did I tell you about Mrs Mandeville?'

'No,' said Linda. She was obviously to get no praise from either man for her achievement.

'Called yesterday evening, I did.' He chuckled. 'She told me to come in the afternoon, of course. Walked in the back door and tiptoed upstairs. There she was in bed with her husband. Such consternation. Don't think she'll invite me again! Great big, dark powerful man, he is. Leapt out of bed as if he'd been shot!'

When the laughter had subsided, Peter looked across at his father with admiration. 'Now *that's* the sort of behaviour of which I entirely approve! Maybe it's going to be more fun in General Practice than I thought.'

'I'll run you to the station if you like,' said Linda.

'Good idea, he's left it late as usual,' said Cooper.

'I'll have my new wheels next time, so no sweat.'

Father and son shook hands with affection, then Linda walked Peter across the yard to her car.

'My father certainly knows how to cope with an awkward situation. You should take notes.'

'Oh, I do,' said Linda. 'I admire him very much.' As they settled into the car, she added, 'Oh, by the way, Mrs Mandeville's husband was in my surgery the other day with some small ailment. He's a short, fair man, actually.'

Peter chuckled appreciatively. Linda cruised out of the yard, then zoomed off down the road.

'I can see you could be a force to be reckoned with,' remarked Peter, and laid his arm along the back of her seat.

CHAPTER THREE

THE CONNOISSEUR

'It looks like 'flu. There's a lot of it about just now. You must stay in bed and –'

'But I'm going to London tomorrow, Grandfather promised!'

'I'm afraid not, my dear.'

Linda looked down at her young patient and saw tears well up in her eyes.

The little girl was small for her ten years and looked lost in the four-poster bed.

'Please, Mrs Dibley!' The child turned appealingly to an elderly woman who stood by her pillow.

'You heard what Doctor Ford said, Erica.'

'Please, Doctor. I'll miss Daddy.'

Linda shook her head and patted Erica's shoulder sympathetically.

The two women walked from the room, Linda giving some medical instructions to Mrs Dibley, who noted them with meticulous care.

'The poor child doesn't get the chance to see her father

much, living so far away; only when her grandfather will take her up – and he doesn't care to very often. Her mother's in America. There was a divorce, you know.'

Mrs Dibley lowered her voice on the last words as they were approaching a pair of elegant double doors.

'Perhaps the visit could be delayed a few days,' suggested Linda. 'She may not get it very badly and –'

'Oh, that wouldn't be possible,' said Mrs Dibley. 'The Commander never changes his plans.'

They had stopped at the doors.

'I wonder if *you* would tell the Commander about his granddaughter, Doctor. I'm sure you would explain it better.'

She's afraid of the old man, thought Linda. And yet she must have been housekeeping for him for years. Amazing.

Linda realised it wasn't so amazing, however, when she was ushered into the gentleman's presence. He stood up as she came in and as he towered over her, straight-backed, and gimlet-eyed, she felt a little awed herself.

'This is Doctor Ford, Commander,' said Mrs Dibley. 'She's just seen Erica. This is Commander Hewson-Laws, Doctor.'

'Ford?'

'How do you do,' said Linda politely. 'I'm here in Stoke Dabenham for six months as Doctor Cooper's locum. When he knew I was calling here at Westbrook House he sent you his regards.'

'Hm. You're very young. Your first experience of General Practice I imagine?'

Linda felt resentment well up in her, although the supposition was, of course, correct.

'Your granddaughter has 'flu, Commander. I understand you were taking her to London tomorrow. She's very disappointed.'

'Can't say the same myself. Blessed girl always gets

car-sick. Well, it can't be helped. You'll take care of her, Mrs Dibley?'

'Of course, sir, doctor's given me all the orders.'

'Anything she needs –'

'Yes, sir. Leave it to me.'

He glanced at Linda and must have read some disapproval in her face, for he added, 'I have an important auction to attend.'

As he spoke he ran his fingers over a jade carving on the desk beside him, and Linda remembered that Doctor Cooper had mentioned the Commander was an antique collector of some distinction.

'I'll be calling again, Mrs Dibley,' said Linda, turning toward the door. 'Good afternoon, Commander.'

'Give my compliments to Doctor Cooper. I'll be away ten days. Tell him we'll have dinner together when I get back.'

Mrs Dibley opened the door for Linda, then turned back.

'There's just one little matter, Commander,' she began.

Linda waited. It was obvious the woman welcomed her presence for moral support.

'What now, Mrs Dibley?'

'My young niece. You had given me permission to have her here while you were both away, you remember, sir?'

'Well?'

'I'm afraid it's rather late to make other arrangements for her.'

'Then she'll have to come, won't she?'

'It's the school holiday and what with her parents being abroad. I'll keep her in my quarters, of course.'

'Yes, yes, Mrs Dibley, I rely on you.'

Thus dismissed, Mrs Dibley showed Linda into the hall.

'Is there nowhere else your niece can go, Mrs Dibley?'

'There isn't, Doctor. I wish there were. Still, Jenny's a sturdy girl.'

'Well, keep her out of the sick-room. We've quite a little epidemic on our hands right now.'

When she went in to surgery that evening, Linda gave John Cooper the Commander's message.

'How did you get on with him?' said Cooper quizzically. 'He's a remarkably interesting man, you know. Nothing he doesn't know about old porcelain. His best pieces are locked away in the long gallery. You must get him to show you sometime.'

'I don't think I'll bother!'

John Cooper smiled.

'I'll insist he includes you in his invitation to dinner, Doctor Ford.'

'Please!' Linda threw up her hands in mock alarm.

'Which reminds me, come to supper Saturday night. My son will be down for the weekend. He keeps me up to date with things, you know.'

This paragon of a medical man who'd never put a foot wrong during his training and passed all his exams with flying colours first time of trying! So they were to be honoured with another visit, Linda thought.

'I'd love to,' said Linda. 'If my cold doesn't develop.'

'Heavens, don't *you* go down with it, girl!'

Linda assured him she wouldn't. Nevertheless, a few days later as she was making her calls, Linda felt an ominous tickling in her throat, her medical bag felt three times its normal weight, and she found herself more than usually sympathetic with her 'flu patients.

At Westbrook House when she called, Erica was much improved and already up and about.

'They can get over things so quickly when they're young,' said Mrs Dibley.

'Yes,' agreed Linda hoarsely. 'But don't let her go outdoors yet awhile.'

44

'No, Doctor. She's not anxious to. She and my niece have struck up a friendship and they're keeping each other amused very nicely.'

As Linda walked up the stairs, Mrs Dibley was called to the telephone. She turned back, gesturing to Linda to carry on.

Hearing children's voices in the distance, Linda continued up and along a landing.

There were several closed doors along the landing, and the voices had suddenly stopped now so that Linda had no idea where the children might be.

She tried a couple of bedrooms without success, then found herself at the end of the corridor faced with a single, impressively carved door. She paused. Behind it she felt sure she could hear whispering. She tried the handle but it didn't give. She listened again and thought she heard a window shut.

'Erica! Are you in there?' said Linda, uncertainly.

It was at this point that Mrs Dibley came hurrying up behind her. She gave a little gasp.

'Those children are surely not in the gallery!' she said. She rattled the door-handle. 'Come out!' she cried. 'Come out this instant!'

They heard a key turn in the lock, and the door opened slowly. There stood the two small figures. Erica looked very red in the face, while Jenny was ashen.

'You know you're not allowed in there! Where did you find the key?'

'I know where Grandfather keeps it.'

'Give it to me. At once!'

Mrs Dibley seized the key from the child and hustling them out of the way, she locked the door. And as she did, Linda was surprised to notice that her hand was trembling.

Jenny had already disappeared below stairs when Linda examined Erica and pronounced her on the mend with no further visits necessary.

But the next morning Mrs Dibley was on the telephone to surgery. 'It's my niece – Jenny. She's had nightmares all night. And her temperature's up. I'm afraid she's got 'flu.'

When Linda got to Westbrook House, it was to find Jenny in bed. She could see at once there was more to Jenny's sickness than 'flu.

'Has something happened to her, Mrs Dibley? She seems to be in a state of shock.'

'Yes,' said the housekeeper, 'I think it has.' She looked worried. 'I'm sure something upset her yesterday, but I don't know what. You remember when I found the two girls in the long gallery?'

'Yes, I do.'

'You won't tell the Commander, will you?'

'Of course not.'

'Well, it was after that, she seemed to be in a terrible state.'

'I wonder if I could have a word with Erica, Mrs Dibley.'

'Yes, of course, come with me.'

Under Linda's questioning, Erica wriggled and hedged evasively.

'Now listen, Erica, we know you were in that gallery and that something frightened Jenny. What was it?'

'A ghost!' said Erica, suddenly. 'We saw a ghost.'

'A ghost? In daylight?'

'Yes, Doctor Ford. It was all dressed in grey and it sort of glided right down the corridor and into the gallery – that's why we went in – then it disappeared. We were *terrified*!'

'Mm,' said Linda. 'You know, I think we'd better investigate this, Mrs Dibley.'

'Oh, it won't be there now,' said Erica, quickly.

'We'll see.'

'Nobody's allowed in the gallery – Grandfather says so!'

Linda looked at Mrs Dibley, who hesitated, then said: 'Well, it so happens the gallery is open for window-cleaning today so –'

'I'm not going! There's a ghost! A ghost!' cried Erica, and ran away down the passage.

The window-cleaner was busily at work when Mrs Dibley and Linda entered the gallery.

Mrs Dibley nodded to him then led Linda down the long room where the Commander's art treasures were housed.

Set out all up and down the room were pieces of delicate and rare china; ornaments, bowls, vessels and figures of all kinds. The sunlight streamed down on the sparkling porcelain, highlighting the colours and setting gold leaf winking.

Linda could see nothing that could have accounted for Jenny's shock. Nothing in the least gruesome or – Suddenly, Mrs Dibley beside her gave a cry and grasped at her arm.

'Oh no!'

'What is it?'

'It's missing.'

'What is?'

'Doctor Ford, there should be a china group over there – three eighteenth-century figures playing musical instruments. It's always been there. Always.'

'Perhaps the Commander has taken it up to London with him,' suggested Linda. But neither of them believed this for a moment.

'But if he hasn't –'

The uncompleted sentence hung in the air, a suspicion dawning on them.

As they left the gallery, the window-cleaner watched them from the corner of his eye, aware of the anxiety in that heavy silence. He well appreciated their apprehension. Hadn't he often suffered under the lash of the Commander's tongue for as little as a smeared window. Poor old Mrs Dibley had a right to be scared. He was terrified of the Commander himself. If it hadn't been that Westbrook House was a considerable job with its many windows, and that he needed the money right now, he'd have left the Commander to his own devices long ago. As it was he just steered clear of him.

And so it was that when he came across the china ornament in the window-box half an hour later, he had no hesitation in leaving it strictly where it was, determined to forget he'd seen those tell-tale pieces.

Mrs Dibley saw Linda out of the front door. The lines on her face seemed deeper.

'I wonder if it's *very* valuable,' she said distractedly.

Linda departed without answering her question. But she knew it was; as she told the assembled company at supper on Saturday evening.

'The poor woman must be worried sick,' said Linda.

'Of course he's crazy about that collection,' said Peter.

'Let's put it this way,' said his father. 'I wouldn't like to be in her shoes when he discovers his loss.'

They had finished eating and decided to take their coffee in the lounge. As they rose, Peter stepped quickly round to pull back Linda's chair for her, and she was strongly aware again of his nearness. With her chill only just conquered she hadn't dared to wear anything too flimsy, so she'd chosen an emerald silk kaftan, embroidered with gold thread. It was exotic; and as her voice was still two tones down the scale, she felt quite glamorous. As long as my nose isn't still rose pink! thought Linda as she caught Peter eyeing her intently again later.

The conversation turned to current films and Linda

realised she'd grown quite out of touch and said so.

'Let's see what's on in Yelchester tomorrow night,' said Peter, reaching for the local newspaper.

'I thought you were going back tomorrow,' remarked his father.

'I'll go up Monday morning,' said Peter quickly. 'What's the position about surgery?'

'Doctor Ford's off duty,' said John Cooper. 'But don't keep her out till dawn. She's had a touch of the plague!'

'Look, I have to see some friends the other side of Yelchester in the afternoon. Could we meet at the Royal Oak for a drink then go on to the film?' asked Peter.

'Thank you. I'd love to,' said Linda, only later realising she hadn't even thought to ask what film was on. It'll make a break, she said to herself. And it'll be no hardship to be squired about for an evening by Peter the Great.

On Sunday evening it was raining. Surgery was over, John Cooper was out on a call and Elsie Peach was manning the telephone, as Linda climbed into her reliable old M.G. and began backing across the yard.

She swung the car round towards the gate, but got no further. A small figure was caught in her headlights.

Linda leapt from her seat and ran forward just in time to catch Jenny in her arms as she fell.

She half-led half-carried the girl across the yard and somehow got her upstairs into her flat. All the time Jenny was shivering and sobbing and clutching at her as if she were drowning.

At last Linda was able to comfort her enough to get a coherent explanation.

'She said I did it! She told Auntie it was me!'
'Who?'
'Erica. She told Auntie that I took the ornament!'

Linda had wrapped a blanket round Jenny and was now busy making her a warm drink.

'You shouldn't have left your bed, you know, dear,' she said, frowning at the child's flushed cheeks.

'I heard them talking. Auntie told Erica she would have to tell the Commander it was missing. So Erica said I took it. But I didn't! I didn't!'

Linda put the weeping girl into her bed where she calmed down a little although she was still in a fever. After a while Linda phoned Elsie Peach and told her to switch the telephone through and come over to the flat.

'I've done all I can for the child for the moment, Elsie. I've been trying to ring Westbrook House but I can't get through. They must be frantic about her. Will you keep an eye on her while I slip up and tell them she's here?'

Elsie nodded and sat down beside Jenny, tenderly mopping her wet forehead.

Mrs Dibley was appalled when she heard what had happened.

'Poor Jenny. Poor little girl. I'd no idea she could hear us talking. Of course she didn't take the ornament. I know that. And Erica only said it because she was afraid. It must have been burglars. I'm sure it was a burglar!'

So that's what she intends to tell the Commander thought Linda. She knows the children are lying, but she's prepared to lie herself to protect them.

When Erica appeared, Linda confronted her with her untruth which she soon admitted.

'It must have been the ghost that took it. We did see a ghost. Honestly we did!' said Erica, frantically changing her story again.

'A ghost,' said Linda. 'Up there?' She pointed to the shadows at the top of the stairs.

'Y–yes,' said Erica.

'What was it like did you say?'

'Erm – all grey. It was in a sort of nun's costume.'

'Really?' Linda peered up the stairs with great interest, then suddenly pointed.

'Heavens yes! It's there now!'

Erica shrieked.

Linda quickly took her hand. 'Oh no,' she said. 'It's only the curtain blowing.'

But Erica had dissolved into tears. She clung to Linda despairingly: 'It was broken! We didn't mean to! Please don't tell Grandfather! Please!'

'What did you do with it?' asked Mrs Dibley, stroking Erica's hair.

But the girl would say no more and Linda passed her over into Mrs Dibley's arms.

'Leave Jenny with me for the time being,' said Linda and Mrs Dibley accepted gratefully.

Driving home, Linda suddenly felt a surge of anger at the whole business. She hurried back to take care of Jenny.

It was several hours later before she remembered she had missed her date at the Royal Oak.

Now I'll *never* know what film was on, she thought ruefully.

In the morning, Peter's newly acquired BMW had gone. Linda hoped he'd got the note she sent via Elsie, apologising for letting him down.

Elsie arrived just before ten at the flat as arranged so that Linda could get off to surgery.

'How's the little girl?'' she asked anxiously.

'Her temperature's down a bit but she's none too bright.'

'I hope you slept all right on that divan bed, Doctor. It looks a right devil.'

'It is – and I've the scars to prove it,' grinned Linda.

'Doctor Cooper says she can come over to the big house in the spare room, just as soon as it's possible.'

'That's very kind of him. I certainly don't think we can send her back to Westbrook House. The Commander's due back tomorrow.'

'Oh my dear life,' proclaimed Elsie. 'Now the fat'll be in the fire!'

It was.

The Collector missed the piece almost at once and came striding out of the long gallery with a face of thunder, calling for Mrs Dibley. Half an hour later she was still standing before him in the study, her hands pressed tight together and her shoulders hunched against the storm.

At last she escaped and made for the telephone.

She came through to Linda on the pretext of asking after her niece but almost at once she broke down and was pouring out everything through broken sobs.

'He said he'd always thought me a responsible woman – that he'd always trusted me – and I'd let him down. He said the articles in the long gallery were in my care and that I should have stopped anyone entering the gallery while he was away. And he just shouted when I mentioned burglars! And as for ghosts! And he said he trusted the window-cleaner because he'd worked here for years. So there was only one person.'

'Who did he mean?' asked Linda.

'My niece, of course! He's asked that her room be searched, and her suitcase! And he even asked if she'd had anything with her when she left so suddenly. That's what's made him so suspicious, you see, her rushing off like that. I'm at my wits end! I told him little Jenny was ill and got frightened and didn't know what she was doing. But he wants her questioned. In fact, he says as soon as she's better he's going to question her himself!'

She dissolved in such a flood of tears that Linda could make out no more of what she was saying. So she made comforting noises and replaced the receiver.

Really the whole thing was getting wildly out of proportion. And that Commander had no right to trample everyone under foot like this. This was the man that Doctor Cooper dined with. Even so, she would tell him all about it when the opportunity arose.

During the ensuing days the story of the missing ornament became village gossip and there was scarcely a house Linda visited where Jenny's health wasn't asked after – which was a good way of leading the conversation round to the mystery.

Then amongst the victims of the 'flu fell the window-cleaner's wife. Linda climbed the dark, boxed-in stairs of their terraced cottage to attend the woman, who had contracted the illness badly.

The window-cleaner stood anxiously by and two subdued young children waited below in the kitchen.

Linda wrote her prescriptions and rose to leave.

'Doctor!'

Linda returned to her patient.

'Is that ornament still missing?'

'Yes, it is.'

The woman looked up with frank and honest eyes. 'Then my husband has something to tell you.'

The window-cleaner looked troubled, and his wife took his hand.

'We must, my dear,' she said. 'No matter what happens. It's only right.' He nodded reluctantly and she went on. 'He found it in a window-box. It's probably still there. He should have said, but he was afraid he'd get the blame. We've both been that worried!'

Linda found herself quite enraged by the fact that, through fear, so many normally honest people had been driven to spin such a web of deceit and mistrust.

Now possessed of the whole facts of the case, she recounted them to Doctor Cooper.

'I suppose you think I ought to "bell the cat",' he said.

'Not at all!' flashed Linda. 'I think I'd quite enjoy telling him.'

'I think you're getting your priorities wrong, Doctor,' observed John Cooper drily. 'The Commander has good reason to be annoyed.'

'Agreed,' said Linda. 'But what has he gained by instilling terror into everyone round him? Just delay in getting at the truth. The children didn't intend to do malicious damage. It was unfortunate and everyone's sorry – but I see no reason why they should be subjected to excessive torment!'

John Cooper took a long look at her and when he spoke his tone was formal.

'Doctor Ford,' he said. 'I have already advised you against getting emotionally involved in the problems of your patients.'

Linda felt ashamed of her outburst. But she had to make her point.

'I know you're right, Doctor Cooper,' she said soberly. 'I also accept your word that the ornament was worth a great deal to the Commander. But people's feelings must surely be respected too, and aren't they equally fragile?'

'I could get down this weekend if you were free to come to dinner.' Peter Cooper was on the telephone to Linda.

'I'm sorry, your father and I have an invitation to Commander Hewson-Laws.'

'You can get out of that, surely?'

'I want to go.'

'You're kidding. First you stand me up at the cinema. O.K. I got the note. And now this. Are you warning me off? I mean seriously?'

'No! We're taking young Jenny back with us as she's

better now, and there's likely to be a scene.'

'Now take my advice, Linda. Don't interfere.'

Oh no, thought Linda, not him too! Why couldn't anyone understand.

'I don't want the Commander upsetting those children any more.'

'You're taking too much on yourself.'

'They're my patients!'

'I suggest you leave it to my father.'

'But the Commander's his friend.'

'That wouldn't prejudice him, I assure you.'

'He won't get involved – he said so.'

'And very right too! Come to dinner with me. I won't be free again for ages, I warn you.'

'I'm sorry.'

On Saturday evening, as she got dressed, Linda felt quite as glum as Jenny, who was miserably gathering her belongings together for the transfer to Westbrook. They all drove over in Doctor Cooper's car and at the door Jenny was quickly spirited away by Mrs Dibley whilst the two doctors went into the study to take sherry with the Commander.

Linda joined in the general conversation on a strictly social level. The two men were soon engaged in the discussion of antiques and Linda lapsed into silence. Despite herself she found the Commander's knowledge and enthusiasm impressive and fascinating.

They went in to dinner. The table was set for three. So Erica was not to eat with them. Still in disgrace probably.

The meal was excellent and the Commander held forth with stories and reminiscences of the strange histories of old works of art. As he talked, his eyes alight and his voice warm with delight in his subject, it gradually dawned on Linda how deeply the man was obsessed with his passion for these treasures, and suddenly she understood something of the rage he had felt at the children's carelessness.

Then Linda became aware that Doctor Cooper had taken over the conversation and was leading it into the realm of the abstract, and the Commander was being invited to dwell on the relative values of inanimate objects as against the human spirit. He caught Linda's eye.

The crafty fellow, she thought, he's on my side after all, as she heard him quietly launch into a simple and straightforward account of the events surrounding the drama of the ornament, and the complications and distress that had grown out of fear of the Commander's anger.

Linda saw the old man's face grow grim as he listened but he stayed quiet until the doctor had finished, then he spoke with difficulty.

'Very well, Cooper, you have made your point. I appreciate that whatever happened was an accident, but what business had those children in my long gallery in the first place!'

'That is a question you might ask them with some profit,' suggested John Cooper.

'Very well,' said the Commander, after a pause, and he sent for the two girls. 'And here is the key to the gallery, Mrs Dibley,' he added. 'Tell them to bring what they put in the window-box.'

Linda felt a pang of pity as the white-faced little figures entered the room. Erica had the pieces of the ornament clutched to her chest.

The Commander rose and turned towards the bookshelf and when he spoke his voice was unsteady. 'Put what you have brought on the table,' he said.

Erica did so, and the two children stood with their eyes fixed on the tall man who remained with his back to them, struggling to control his temper.

In the pause, Linda glanced at John Cooper and saw him take up the three tiny china heads and set them into the sockets which formed their necks. He looked up at her triumphantly. It was obvious the heads were meant to be loose. The piece wasn't broken at all!

Linda opened her mouth to speak, but the doctor gestured her to silence. The Commander was speaking.

'Erica, why did you go into the long gallery?'

'Because I wanted to show Jenny the lovely things,' said Erica, simply. 'Because they're so beautiful.'

There was another silence as the Commander absorbed the implication of her words.

Drawing on all her courage, Jenny spoke up. 'We're very, very sorry, sir. Truly.'

'Honestly, Grandfather,' added Erica. 'I know you loved it. And – and it was so pretty!' She burst into tears.

'I accept your apology,' said the Commander, and though stiff, his voice was not cold.

Only then did John Cooper speak.

'Surely, Commander, this isn't broken is it?' he said innocently.

It was true. The delicate heads were separate pieces, designed to move when stirred by a draught, as the Commander took great pleasure in explaining.

The two children were enraptured as the old collector set the piece in motion and the tiny musicians appeared to nod in time as they played.

'I never knew!' cried Erica. Then she frowned. 'But of course there's no breeze in the long gallery.'

The Commander looked down at the two girls as they bent over the ornament, smiling delightedly.

'I won't put it back there,' he said. 'We'll have it out on the grand piano in the sitting room. Then in the summer, when the windows are open, we'll all enjoy it.'

Later as Mrs Dibley showed the two doctors out, she

touched John Cooper's arm. 'Thank you, Doctor,' she said, 'for handling the matter.'

Just as well it wasn't left to me, thought Linda, or right now we'd be fleeing down the drive with the Commander pursuing us with a genuine fifteenth-century gilt-inlaid double-barrelled blunderbuss!

CHAPTER FOUR

KITH AND KIN

The level-crossing was closed.

Linda stopped her car and, as she sat waiting, thumbed through the file of one of the patients she had just visited. There were certain symptoms that puzzled her and she made a note to look them up immediately she got back to the surgery. This failing to help, she'd talk to Doctor Cooper, who was always prepared to give her the benefit of his long experience.

A freight train trundled past and the gates shuddered open again. Linda drove through. As she did, she glanced automatically along the line and saw two small boys scrambling down the bank. She suspected at once the game they were playing.

Parking the car safely she got out and went back, but as she walked along the verge towards them, they ran away, leaving two flattened pennies behind as evidence that she had been right about their occupation. Linda followed the boys up the bank and sprinted across a field after them. She'd been athletics champion of her school and was gratified to find she still had a useful burst of speed.

The boys disappeared round the back of an old shed and when Linda reached it were nowhere to be seen. A suppressed scuffling, however, gave them away, and Linda realised they had taken refuge on the roof of the hut.

'Now listen to me, lads, that's a very dangerous game, playing about on the railway line.' Linda spoke with authority. Hadn't she, as a child, been the ringleader in most of the mischief her gang had got into?

'I know it's fun but you'd be amazed how fast –' A sharp cry stopped her.

'Here, miss, look, quick!'

The interruption was so urgent that Linda took it seriously.

'What's the matter?'

'There's someone dead in this shed!'

The second boy spoke: 'Yes! We can see him through this window on the roof!' Their voices were shrill with fright.

The boys climbed down and joined Linda at the door of the shed, where she knocked, then tried the handle. It was locked. As she rattled at it, they all heard the low growl of a dog coming from inside. It was the deep-throated warning of a large animal and the boys wriggled with alarm. Linda was relieved that they did not desert her.

'It's an old man, lying on the floor, miss, all white.'

They were patently telling the truth.

'We must break in,' said Linda. The boys' eyes lit up with excitement and they joined in the operation with enthusiasm.

It was not difficult, for the wood was rotten, and as the door swung open, Linda could see the figure lying on the floor, obviously fallen out of a turned-over camp cot.

The hut was roughly furnished as a dwelling and apart from the heap of dingy bedding looked simple but orderly.

All this they observed instantly, but before anyone could move, a great dog had leapt forward and planted itself between them and the body of the old man.

It was a brown dog, a cross perhaps between a Retriever and Alsatian. Its shoulders were powerful and right now its lips were curled back over its teeth in an ominous snarl. There was no doubt it intended to defend its master against all comers. It lunged and the boys squealed and dodged back.

Linda went for help.

An hour later, an RSPCA officer had secured the dog with a loop and rod; and ambulance men were able to load the man onto a stretcher.

The two boys had remained glued to the scene throughout.

'He's not dead,' said Linda. 'Not quite. Do you know him?'

They shook their heads, and watched as the frail figure was borne off on the first part of its journey to Yelchester Cottage Hospital.

As the doors of the ambulance slammed to, the dog squirmed violently and broke free. It stood an instant in indecision then turned and streaked away across the countryside.

The old man had pneumonia and was suffering from malnutrition and neglect, but he began to recover slowly.

'He's obviously been living as a complete recluse,' said the Matron to Linda. 'He's a well-spoken man and everyone likes him, but we can't get him to name any relative or friends who might be concerned about him. Would you have a word with him? He says his name is Henry Prowse.'

But Linda was no luckier. Although he was otherwise

friendly he was not to be drawn about his background. His main concern was about his dog. He was very upset and worried about it and when he found Linda knew what it looked like he begged her to keep watch for it on her rounds.

Linda felt sorry that the old man should have lost his only living companion and a day or two later she drove out specially to look round the area, starting at the broken-down shed.

The place had been stripped of all the man's smaller possessions, which had been taken away for safe-keeping, and it looked damp and derelict. The dog was not there; but in poking about under the bed to make sure, Linda came across a photograph which immediately caught her interest. It had been cut out of a newspaper and was of a man of about fifty, well-dressed and important-looking, and strongly resembling the old man in the Cottage Hospital.

Thoughtfully, Linda tucked it into her handbag.

She went back to the car and drove round the lanes, stopping at one or two cottages to make enquiries about the dog. Eventually she found someone who thought they knew where it was and directed her to a ramshackle little dwelling hidden in a spinney.

At her knock there was a hurried scuffle inside and a furtive movement of curtains, then the door opened. A lean, weathered man stood in tattered breeches and faded woollen shirt, smiling enquiringly. Behind him, Linda could see a woman stooping over a baby in a cot, three other children – two of whom were the boys from the railway line – and a young man of about twenty who was lurking in a corner. All the faces were turned towards her with interest.

The old man's dog rose up from the hearth and joined the audience, wagging its tail welcomingly.

For the next half hour, Linda was entertained most

hospitably. It seemed the boys had found the dog in an exhausted condition and brought it home, where it had settled down with the family. The man of the house, who introduced himself as Tom Greenway, presented his wife who gave Linda a drink of tea in a chipped enamel mug and – when she knew Linda was a doctor – took the opportunity to consult her on the children's health. The youngsters grinned at her cheerfully as she checked them over, discovering that apart from several layers of grime they all appeared to be in perfect condition. The young man was introduced as Joe, a nephew from London.

It was chaotic but there was genuine warmth about the place and Mrs Greenway was upset that nobody had known about the lonely old man, and at once offered to care for his dog until he was well.

This seemed a good idea and Linda accepted; she rose. Suddenly there was a knock at the door, and she was amazed to see the whole family immediately riveted with apprehension.

Tom Greenway stepped to the window and peered out, then turning he made a quick gesture towards Joe, who promptly shot out of the back exit with the silent speed of a rodent.

When the front door was opened it revealed a policeman on the threshold. It was the local man from Stoke Dabenham and he recognised Linda. He passed the time of day with her as she took her leave, then turned to Tom Greenway.

'I wonder if I could have a word with you, Mr Greenway,' she heard him saying heavily, as she went off through the trees.

That evening Doctor Cooper invited her over to the big house for a drink after surgery, and was highly amused by the story.

'Tom Greenway,' he chuckled, 'comes from a long

line of villains. He's the straightest of the lot – and he's a poacher!'

'I rather liked them,' said Linda. 'And the children are happy and bonny enough.'

'So they should be – living off Colonel Holroyd's pheasant!'

'Anyway old Mr Prowse will be delighted about his dog. It's quite happy and they'll look after it till he comes out of hospital. Though what's to become of him then I wonder? He can't go back to that shack.'

'An Old People's Home.'

Linda frowned.

'There's a very pleasant one at –'

'Oh, I'm sure,' said Linda. But she was thinking of that dog.

John Cooper refilled her glass, then cut across her thoughts by reaching a gilt-edged card down from the mantelpiece and waving it in front of her.

'Enough shop-talk,' he said, 'are you still interested in going to this?'

It was an invitation to a Chamber of Trade Ball in Plymouth. The two doctors had each had an invitation.

'My son Peter's coming down that weekend and if you've no other partner you'd like to take, I suggest you might go together. How do you feel about that?'

'Why don't we all go,' said Linda.

Linda drove over to Yelchester to get her curls tamed and buy a new lipstick for the Ball. The hairdresser lifted her thick shiny hair into a Grecian style. A few tendrils escaped and softened the line round her face. Linda regarded the effect as satisfactory and was gratified when she received admiring looks as she walked through the corridors of the Cottage Hospital, she was making a quick call on Mr Prowse to set his mind at rest about the dog.

The old man was so grateful and relieved that Linda was more than glad she'd taken the trouble. Nevertheless, when she showed him the photograph she had found in the hut, he at once became withdrawn and gave her only evasive answers about it.

Linda's dress was white chiffon printed with an art nouveau pattern of flowers at the hem. It had been an extravagance designed to please that other young man before she had discovered he was lost to her. She had not worn the dress since. But the memory was fading and as she and Peter set off for Plymouth, she was aware that they made an elegant couple and she was all set for an enjoyable evening.

John Cooper had decided not to go in the end, but his son knew a great many people present and obviously enjoyed introducing Linda to them. Soon they were part of a large, friendly group, laughing and talking noisily.

Then, across the dance floor, Linda saw a familiar face. For a moment she thought it must be someone she knew, then realised with a shock where she had seen the man before. There was no doubt whatever, it was on the scrap of newspaper she'd taken from the hut.

'Who is that man?' she asked, urgently.

'I've no idea,' said Peter Cooper.

'Can you find out?'

Peter dutifully moved off to make some enquiries and returned a few minutes later to inform Linda that the gentleman in question was a very important local executive who owned a chain of launderettes and dry cleaners, also a typing agency and employment bureau, and three supermarkets. His first wife had died some years ago and he'd married a wealthy Plymouth girl.

'He's a very big potato indeed hereabouts.'

'Yes,' said Linda, 'but his name? What's his name?'

'Prowse.'

Linda told Peter about the old man in the hospital.

Reluctantly he agreed that she should have a word with the younger Mr Prowse who was at that moment dancing past with a smart, young, fair-haired woman in blue.

When the music finished Linda went over to the man and asked if she could talk to him in the adjoining lobby. The woman accompanied him and Peter joined them at Linda's request.

When they had all introduced themselves, the man ordered some drinks then turned to Linda smiling in polite enquiry.

But as Linda broke the news to him about old Mr Prowse his expression changed, hardening into formality.

'Yes. It must be my father,' he said. 'I lost touch with him some time ago.'

'He's practically better now,' said Linda. 'After being *very* ill.'

'I'm glad,' said Prowse, without emotion.

'There's some concern about what will happen to him when he comes out of hospital.'

Linda waited. Prowse did not speak, so she went on.

'There are Old Folks' Homes of course –'

Still no reaction.

'But there's the question of his dog, and he's very anxious to keep it.'

At last the man spoke. 'I suppose you think I should offer him a home with us, but it's not that simple. We have a comparatively small house and in any case I do a great deal of entertaining and my spare rooms are used by guests most of the time.'

'In any case, Charles,' said his wife, 'a dog would be quite impossible.' She turned her large blue eyes on Peter. 'I have three already, and they've been most dreadfully spoiled and I'm afraid they're not in the least friendly to other dogs. You know how it is.'

'That's a fact,' said Prowse, smiling indulgently at Mrs Prowse. 'No, I really don't see it being convenient to have the old chap at home. But of course we will do everything we can to help otherwise, won't we Melinda?'

'Oh naturally!' said the young woman, nodding her blonde head emphatically and making to rise.

'I'll take your address, if I may,' said Linda. 'And ask Matron to get in touch with you.'

'Such enthusiasm at finding his long-lost dad,' said Linda.

Peter drew her on to the dance floor. 'My darling girl, *do* switch off – just for tonight.'

Linda found she rather liked that light term of endearment. And she had no aversion to the arm that was holding her closer than was strictly necessary.

Over Peter's shoulder she glimpsed the man Prowse dancing with his wife – their feet in perfect accord – their faces scowling angrily at each other.

'I wonder what the real story is behind it all,' said Linda.

'Behind what, dear heart? Life?'

'No, the Prowses.'

'I do not know. And right now I do not care!' announced Peter, and his arm loosened around her.

'All right. All right,' said Linda, and tickled the back of his neck.

Peter grinned at her. Then the music changed to a quicker mood, and they parted to dance separately to the beat.

Linda had to leave it there.

She and Peter rejoined their party and thereafter danced the night away.

At her door Peter kissed her goodnight. It was a light kiss but it made her tremble. He stepped back from her, and hesitated. They were both quite still. Poised. Then he made off quickly into the dark.

Linda had expected something more demonstrative – felt sure he had intended more – yet that moment standing there silently in key with each other had been oddly pleasing. And intriguing. Which is probably what he intended! she thought, as she put herself under a cool shower.

A few days later a letter came to the hospital from Charles Prowse, offering a generous sum to support his father. The Matron told Linda about it on the telephone.

'But it's no good, Doctor Ford,' she said. 'The old boy will have none of it.'

'Oh dear.'

'I finally got the story out of him. It seems old Mr Prowse sold up his house fifteen years ago to finance his son in a business venture, throwing in all his savings to get the young man well started.'

'He made good all right!' said Linda.

'Very likely, but do you know he never repaid his debt nor got in touch with his father from that day to this!'

'No wonder the old fellow doesn't want to know him.'

'He refused the money point blank and says he doesn't want anything more to do with his family in any way.'

'But where's he to go?'

'Heaven knows. He'll be out of here in a couple of days and insists on making his own way.'

Later, Linda talked to Doctor Cooper about the matter.

'It's outrageous!' she said angrily. 'It's quite obvious there's more than enough room for the old man in his son's house. They just don't want the bother of him. Afraid it might complicate their social scene, I suppose!'

'People aren't obliged to house their elderly relatives, you know.'

'More's the pity!' flashed Linda.

'Rubbish! It's by no means always the best thing. I suspect old Mr Prowse might have been utterly miserable living with his son.'

'There's such a thing as family feeling,' said Linda, 'look at Tom Greenway. He didn't hesitate to shelter his nephew from the police – though it was a dangerous thing to do.'

'I would say the Greenways are a special case,' observed John Cooper wryly.

'They're loyal to each other and goodhearted,' defended Linda. 'I know you think I'm emotional and idealistic, Doctor Cooper.'

'I do.'

'But I just see an old man and his dog with no home to go to.'

At this moment a call came through from Mrs Perry at the surgery, and both the doctors rose to go off on visits to patients.

Despite Linda's anxiety, old Mr Prowse did find a home to go to when he was discharged. The Greenways offered him accommodation with them, which he accepted, moving his small collection of neat belongings into the cottage, where they were rapidly absorbed into the general confusion.

Some weeks later as Linda was tidying the stable flat she heard the familiar screech of brakes down on the cobbles and looked out to see Peter Cooper's car come to a halt in the yard. Knowing that his father had gone to a meeting, she called out of the window inviting him to come in for a coffee. He accepted enthusiastically and climbed the stairs, smoothing back his hair which was standing on end from the wind.

'It was such good weather,' he said, 'I thought I'd pop down and see how the boss was doing.'

He settled back in the chintz-covered sofa and began

talking about his work in the hospital, in which he was obviously deeply interested. Linda wondered whether John Cooper would ever lure his son down to join him in this country practice, and was surprised to feel quite a pang at the thought that if he did it would mean that she would go. She knew she was temporary but she also knew she was getting very attached to the place.

'I enjoyed that Ball in Plymouth,' Peter was saying, 'even if we did get bogged down a bit by your over-active sense of responsibility.'

He smiled and Linda grinned back ruefully. 'Am I allowed to tell you the latest developments?' she asked.

'If you must. And you obviously must!'

'It's a squalid little cottage and wildly overcrowded but at least the Greenways made him welcome.'

'Thank goodness for that!' said Peter cheerfully, 'now maybe everybody will leave the poor old chap alone as he wants – instead of fussing over his welfare.'

'But –' began Linda.

'He wants to be independent. Stop interfering! Is it possible there's a sandwich lying about the place?'

'Are you hungry? I'll make you one.'

'I knew you'd be concerned for my welfare,' he said, and stretched out to rest as Linda made for the kitchen with a laugh.

When he'd finished a tidy tea, Peter went over to the big house. Linda was called out to a farm accident the other side of Pretting and when she got back the Coopers had gone off to some friends for the evening. She took surgery and did not see anything of them again until the next day, when Peter came over to tell her that there had been a visit the previous evening while Linda was out.

'And who do you think it was?'

'I give up.'

'That old Mr Prowse's granddaughter. I thought you'd be surprised. Lucky I knew all about it as no-one was here. The daughter by Charles Prowse's first wife, so she said. Anyway she introduced herself and said she'd heard her grandfather was ill and she wanted to contact him. Sharp little piece, she was. Been to the hospital but couldn't get his address from them.'

'What did you tell her?' asked Linda, with interest.

'I told her that her grandfather had expressed the wish not to see any of his family again and advised her to leave it at that.'

'You did what!'

'The old boy doesn't want troubling, you know that. For that matter I'd no idea of his address anyway.'

Linda was speechless. But only temporarily. 'You astound me!' she announced. 'If that isn't interfering in the old man's affairs, what is!'

'He said he didn't want –'

'That's not the point. He should have been allowed to tell her himself if he didn't want to see her. It's a great pity you don't practise what you are at such pains to preach!'

'For God's sake!' Peter rose angrily. 'I can't be doing with all this personal involvement. It gets in the way of efficiency – as you'll discover one day, Linda. And the sooner the better for this Practice!' He strode back to the big house, and Linda let him go willingly.

She began preparing her Sunday lunch, digging out the eyes of a potato quite savagely. But by the time it was all cooking, she had pushed the matter aside. She spent a pleasant half hour attending to her pot-plants then ate her meal with a medical journal propped up in front of her.

The afternoon passed with letter writing and practice on John Cooper's old mandolin which he had entrusted to her. She was off surgery and looking forward to a restful evening watching T.V.

Then the bell rang.

Linda trotted down the wooden stairs to the yard.

At the lower door stood a young woman about the same age as Linda. She was dressed in a trouser suit which looked very smart on her tall slim figure. Her jaw was set aggressively and when she spoke her voice was determined.

'Doctor Ford?'

Linda nodded.

'I was sent over from the big house. I hope you're going to be able to help me. I'm Delia Parr and I'm trying to trace my grandfather, Henry Prowse. I've been to the hospital where he was ill recently and I called here yesterday – both with no success. I've come back because I'm quite sure someone must know something of his whereabouts and I do not intend to be fobbed off!'

This is all the old man needs, thought Linda, and then thought guiltily about her spat with Peter. Now she understood.

She felt like telling the girl to get lost herself! But she began politely.

'It's like this, Miss Parr –'

'Mrs.'

'Mrs Parr. Mr Prowse has said he doesn't want to have any more to do with his family. That's why, perhaps, no-one's been very helpful.'

'Do you know his address?'

'Yes I do.'

'Please give it to me.'

Of course I must, thought Linda. I've no right whatever to withhold it. She hesitated a moment trying to think how she was to describe the way to the spinney.

The woman, aware of Linda's reluctance, and mistaking the pause for a refusal, spoke again. But this time her voice was pleading.

'Please! I've been here two days searching. I must go home this evening. I've left my two little girls with my husband but he has to work tomorrow, so I've no more time.'

Linda could suddenly see that the face was tired and anxious under its careful make-up.

'Mr Prowse is living with a family called Greenway. It's a bit off the beaten track, I'm afraid.'

'Whereabouts?'

'Your grandfather has already been offered money, you know, and he refused it,' Linda warned.

'I know!' Her voice was cold again, but not towards Linda.

'Have you got a car?'

'No, I came by train.'

'Oh.' Linda made a decision. 'Look here, I'd better run you there.'

'I don't want to trouble you like that.'

'You'll get lost for sure if I don't,' said Linda briskly. 'Wait here, I just have to slip over to surgery. I'm not busy and it's not that far – just awkward.'

Linda went over to tell Mrs Perry where she was going. She could have phoned through but she rather hoped to catch sight of Peter and make peace. But no luck. Oh well.

John Cooper was just emerging from his consulting room.

'I sent that young person over to you,' he said. 'Tough as nails, that one. The old boy certainly has a charming family!'

'I think she was just determined to find him,' said Linda.

'Well, she'll get a fair surprise when she does. I predict our swinging young lady will disappear as smartly as she came when she encounters the Greenway menage, which I imagine will be something of a shock.'

It was. Linda could see that the moment the cottage door opened. Even before, as they picked their way under a line of half-hearted washing, Delia Parr grimaced.

Mrs Greenway stood smiling at the entrance, the fragrance of old cabbage lingering about her. She greeted Linda warmly.

'I'm afraid my Tom's gone off with Joe in the old van; showing him round the countryside before he goes back to London tonight.'

'No, it's not Mr Greenway, it's Mr Prowse we've come to see.'

'Is it now? Well, step inside, I'm sure.'

Linda went on, 'Perhaps you'd tell him his granddaughter has come to call.'

'I will. He's just out the back.'

She hurried off and the two visitors moved into the centre of the living room. Out of the corner of her eye Linda observed Delia Parr glancing round the room, taking in its peeling wallpaper – the pattern enlivened by childish graffiti; its battered furniture and rubbish-strewn floor, amongst which the three children were playing. The two boys were pulling the baby around on an old rug – a game which raised shrieks of laughter and clouds of dust. The ceiling was low and yellow with grease and smoke that had also taken toll of the curtains which had once perhaps been green.

Delia Parr's face had whitened.

The old man came in, blinking through the gloom, and followed by the dog. He stopped dead.

'Edith!'

'No, Granddad, it's Delia.'

He stared bewildered. 'Edith's girl, oh yes.' His eyes clouded over. 'You've grown up so like her. So like her.'

'*You* haven't changed at all.'

That's hardly true, thought Linda, even since I saw him in hospital, he's quite different. The spruce old man had become grimy and unkempt.

The pair were sitting now and the old man was recalling shared memories. The dog squatted between his knees.

'I'll wait for you in the car,' said Linda, and slipped out

She didn't have to wait long. Delia Parr got into the car without a word, slamming the door. Linda was aware she was shuddering.

'The station?' queried Linda, and received a curt nod. They set off.

So Doctor Cooper *had* been right. The scene had been distasteful and Mrs Parr was taking to her heels.

No further words were exchanged as Linda drove grim-faced to Stoke Dabenham. She was seething. All right, so the Greenways were a mucky lot and feckless, but they were warm-hearted and good-natured; with probably more family solidarity on their hearth than the Prowses would ever know! With some difficulty Linda restrained herself from proclaiming this fact. Instead, when they reached the station and drew up, she merely remarked: 'I thought perhaps you had come to fetch your grandfather. I've been rather concerned about him.'

'And so I *had*. So I *had*!'

The words were so charged with emotion that Linda turned to look at the girl. Tears were running down her face.

'How could my father have done it?' She put her face in her hands. After a moment, she blew her nose and her chin grew firm again. 'I came to take him home to live with us,' she said.

'Then why didn't you?'

'That's a happy home in the spinney, Doctor Ford.'

'It is.'

'For all it's no palace, he's content there. He must have a chance to think about it: the chance to refuse me with dignity if he'd sooner stay with the Greenways.'

Linda could see she was sincere.

'Would you do something else for me, Doctor?'

'Of course.'

'Take a message to him telling him there's room for him with us, and that my husband and children and I all want him very much.'

'But the dog,' queried Linda quickly. 'Will you take it too?'

'Whyever not?' said Delia Parr, as if it was a silly question.

'Tell him I'll wait here till the last train goes.'

Linda weaved her way along the narrow track through the trees towards the cottage.

If only the old man has sense enough to see this offer is worthwhile, she hoped, and doesn't go all stubborn and proud! If only he realises that his granddaughter is offering him affection and respect.

Linda walked old Mr Prowse out into the darkened garden and gave him the message quite simply, and without offering her own opinion.

'Well, Mr Prowse,' she finished, 'is the answer yes or no?'

The old man turned on his heel. 'Come on!' he said and hurried indoors, calling out loudly for a clean shirt.

Linda followed and found everyone diligently searching the house.

'I'll pack up my few traps while you find me that collar, Mrs Greenway, I'm going home with my granddaughter. And Buster too! You're coming, old chap!'

'Oh that's lovely for you, Mr Prowse,' said Mrs Greenway with pleasure, 'she seemed such a nice girl. Now I washed that blue shirt, I know I did.' She began hunting vaguely through a pile of biscuit tins. 'Alfie, give doggie a brush and try and find his lead.'

'You will give Mr Greenway my regards,' said Mr

Prowse, 'and thank you both for your kind hospitality. Have I paid you up to date?'

He settled his affairs and donated a coin each to the children.

The shirt had still not come to light, and Alfie was driving the dog frantic with the hearth-brush.

'I'll do that,' said Linda, feeling out of things. 'You find Mr Prowse's belongings.'

The old man located his raincoat and struggled into it. His shoelace broke and a fresh search was started for another; and a piece of string to secure the dog.

Linda began to get anxious about the time, but at last they got away, leaving the Greenways grouped at the door, shouting and waving farewells.

Driving as fast as she dared, Linda aimed them for the station. Suppose the train had gone, after all this!

It hadn't. But it was at the platform and Linda bundled her passenger out and delivered him, dog and baggage, to his granddaughter, who hastily hauled everything on board. All three were giggling with relief.

As Linda stepped back and the whistle blew, a figure brushed against her, bumping her with a heavy suitcase.

'Beg pardon,' said Tom Greenway's nephew Joe, and leapt on to the train.

Brimming with goodwill, Linda waved him off too.

She was humming as she made her way home. End of story, she thought, and a happy one too. She was not prepared for the other little drama awaiting her.

Doctor Cooper was standing on the doorstep with the local constable. He beckoned her over. It seemed that whilst she'd been out and he'd been busy in surgery, someone had broken into the house.

'But I happened to go through for my other spectacles and disturbed him, so he didn't get away with anything. Saw him beetling down the garden.'

'Good Lord!' said Linda, then waited, suspecting

from Cooper's expression that there was more to come.

'Guess who it was?' he said.

'Er – who?'

'Joe Greenway.'

Linda remembered the heavy suitcase.

'No surprise,' added the constable. 'He usually comes down when things get too hot in London. Lays low with his relations for a bit, then has a quick whip round the district and scarpers up to the smoke again.'

John Cooper looked at Linda quizzically.

'Family solidarity,' he remarked.

That evening Peter apologised.

'I'm truly sorry, Linda. I was quite rude to you.'

'You were.'

'I said unfair things.'

'Yes, I think you did.'

'I've felt wretched since.'

'You'll be able to handle things your way once you're working down here, Peter. But meantime, I have to do what I believe to be best. And to have someone popping down on flying visits trying to tell me how I should behave –'

Peter nodded in agreement. His head was bowed in contrition.

But when he glanced up, his eyes were twinkling.

'You see, Linda, I never used to come down so often. Something keeps drawing me down lately. Can't imagine what it is.'

'Nor can I,' said Linda. 'I'd hate to think it was just to bully me.'

'Be kind to me, Linda. Be forgiving. I'm off to foreign parts tomorrow, who knows what might befall me.'

'Oh. For long?'

At once he'd taken her hand.

'Ages! A week! New York is a terribly dangerous city. I could be mugged, robbed of all I possess –'

'If I know you, they'd end up giving you all *they* possess. You'll have a ball in New York.'

'It's a *conference*, Linda.'

'That won't stop you.'

'You're right. Come with me!'

'Oh Peter!'

'All right. Reject me – spurn me – but say I'm forgiven.'

He stood looking so abject and appealing that Linda laughed and threw her arms around him.

'Have a nice trip,' she said.

Peter kissed her warmly. 'See *you* when I get back,' he said, meaningfully. Then throwing her a wink over his shoulder, he marched off.

Linda watched him out of sight. A whole week in New York. He could meet *anybody*.

CHAPTER FIVE

THE MARTYRS

Linda Ford and John Cooper stood just inside the door of the waiting room and surveyed it critically. The painter climbed down off his ladder and joined them. With a flourish of his brush he presented his handiwork to the two doctors.

'Like it, sir?'

John Cooper turned to Linda.

'I hope you're right about the colour.'

'You wait, Doctor Cooper. It's going to look very elegant and cheerful,' said Linda firmly. At least this was an area where she felt more than a match for the senior doctor. The mushroom walls and white woodwork already gave her pleasure, and she was quite looking forward to putting up the new apricot curtains they were having made.

'I think Doctor Ford's right, sir. I've got to agree. Yes, very nice choice it's turned out,' said Bill Mullett, and mounted his ladder again. He was a pleasant young man, but the cheerful confidence of his manner was somewhat belied by a muscular twitch under his eye.

'He's making a good job of that,' said Linda, as she and Doctor Cooper walked through to the hall.

'Keen to please,' said Cooper. 'He's recently started in business on his own.'

'Pity about that nervous tick under his eye. It's only recent I believe.'

'Yes. Probably anxious about his work. Or maybe there's a domestic problem.'

'Oh not that, I think,' said Linda quickly. 'It's a happy little household. I've attended the baby.'

'Doesn't the mother-in-law live with them?'

'Yes, but she's the kindest little body and devoted to them all.'

'Well. Then let's hope his venture prospers,' commented John Cooper, and went into his study.

Linda was on her way back to her flat over the old stables, when she met Miss Andrews delivering the new curtains. Her frail figure stooped with its burden and Linda hurried to take it.

'You shouldn't have carried them, Miss Andrews.'

'It was nothing, Doctor – just from the other end of the village.'

Linda knew Miss Andrews had a brother who lived at home and wondered why he couldn't have done the job.

'I do hope they're all right. Such a happy colour.'

'What have you done to your finger, Miss Andrews?' asked Linda, noticing the rough bandage.

'Tch! I ran the needle through it.' Then seeing Linda's frown she smiled. 'Oh Doctor, you're not a proper seamstress until you've run the needle through yourself a couple of times!'

'You'd better let me take a look.'

'It's quite all right. I only wrapped it up because my brother can't stand the sight of anything like that.'

'Nevertheless.' Linda led her into the surgery.

It was a nasty jag and the nail was rapidly blackening. After it was dressed, Linda gave Miss Andrews a tetanus injection, and was startled at the thinness of the woman's limbs.

'Phew!' exclaimed Miss Andrews, weakly, smoothing back a grey hair. Then she pulled herself together and put on her coat.

As she was leaving, Bill Mullett was packing up to slip home for his lunch, and offered to drop her off at the wisteria-hung house where she lived.

'Time you had it painted,' said Bill jovially.

'Oh I don't think I could afford it,' said Miss Andrews regretfully.

'Pity to let a nice place like that deteriorate.'

He wasn't just seeking work, he was right, Linda knew. Miss Andrews' house was a small Georgian gem, and Linda always admired it when she drove past.

As the van swerved out of the gate, Miss Andrews clinging to the upholstery, John Cooper emerged from his study.

'Linda!'

Linda went back into the hall.

'Was that Miss Andrews I just saw in the drive?'

'Yes. She was delivering the curtains.'

'She doesn't look well.'

'She's certainly very thin. Has she always been like that?'

'She was never a robust build even as a girl but now – she wears herself out looking after that brother of hers.'

Linda looked at Cooper curiously. It wasn't like him to appear interested in his patients' personal lives, although she suspected his concern went deeper than he ever revealed.

'I know the family well,' he explained, seeing her expression. 'Mary Andrews was a very lovely girl and

I've seen her wither away to a lonely, exhausted woman in her efforts to satisfy Stuart. She waits on him hand and foot, and if ever a man took advantage of a sister's devotion!' John Cooper broke off angrily.

He turned and retreated into his study. Linda was startled. It was the first time she had seen Doctor Cooper lose his usual calm control.

A few days later, Bill Mullett, who was now working on outdoor window-frames, came in to see Linda. His mother-in-law had taken to her bed with pains in the chest and he was worried about her. Linda said she'd call.

'Thanks,' said Bill. 'Here, by the way, I took a bit of sewing round to Miss Andrews this morning – the wife wants some new loose covers – and that finger of hers looks festered to me.'

'She hasn't been in about it,' said Linda.

'She wouldn't – till it dropped off! I just thought I'd mention it.'

'I'll be seeing her today to settle for the curtains, so I'll check that finger at the same time.'

Later it occurred to Linda that John Cooper might like to make this particular call himself and she suggested it.

'Out of the question,' he said shortly. 'I'm the last person welcome in that household!'

Linda knocked on the door, appreciating the elegant brass dolphin that formed the knocker.

After a moment, the door swung open and a man stood before her. He was small-eared and pale-eyed and he leant on a walking stick.

He looked down at the envelope in Linda's hand, rightly surmised what it was, and held out his hand with a brief nod.

'I'd rather like to see Miss Andrews, if I may,' said Linda.

'My sister is busy.'

'It won't take a moment.'

The man hesitated an instant, then stepped aside for Linda to enter and called back into the house.

Mary Andrews came out of a side room with a distracted air, a pair of scissors in her hand. When she saw who it was she showed Linda into a charming lounge. Stuart Andrews followed and seated himself in a deep chair by the French windows where the sun played round his head like a halo, ill fitting his scowling face.

Linda was soon attending to Miss Andrews' finger.

'A spot of penicillin will probably clear it up in no time. You were foolish not to come and see me.'

'I know,' said Miss Andrews, 'but I've so much work outstanding, I couldn't find a minute.'

Linda turned to Stuart. 'If it's no better in a couple of days, you must send her along.'

'She does as she likes,' he said ungraciously.

Linda packed up her bag. She glanced round the room. 'This really is a delightful house, Miss Andrews. You must be very fond of it.'

Mary Andrews shot an alarmed look towards her brother.

'Yes,' she said. 'Yes, indeed.'

'It's the most beautiful house in the village,' said Stuart. '*She* never appreciated it.'

'That's not true, Stuart,' said Miss Andrews. 'It's a fact I never understood its architectural value, but it was home.'

'Home!' He spat out the word, and his sister sighed.

'I've told you a million times, my dear, I don't know why mother left it to me and not you.'

'She always said it was to be mine.'

'She did.' Miss Andrews turned to Linda. 'We'll never know why she changed her mind. When Stuart came home from the lawyers and said it was mine, I was absolutely astounded. I only wish there'd been a little money to go with it; to keep it as we'd like to,' she said ruefully.

'I'll never forgive her.'

Miss Andrews looked at him with gentle reproach. 'Don't speak like that, Stuart. After all you've not really lost anything. You've gone on living here and you know you always can. And I've done my best to make up to you for everything.'

The man turned away with a shrug. Miss Andrews began showing Linda to the door.

'It was a terrible disappointment to him,' she said, her eyes begging Linda to understand and forgive her brother's churlishness.

The problem of property had never crossed Linda's horizon but she supposed that people could dream of ownership and long for possession of a dwelling to which they were particularly devoted.

She volunteered as much to Doctor Cooper that evening when they were drinking coffee together after surgery. But he would have none of it.

'Stuart Andrews is a selfish, twisted man.'

'I suppose he was particularly attached to his mother and felt she betrayed him,' suggested Linda.

'She was certainly devoted to him and it was always a mystery why she left the house to Mary and not him, for she definitely favoured him – though why I can't imagine, he was always a beastly chap.'

'He bears a terrible grudge, anyone can see that,' said Linda. 'What's wrong with his leg?'

'It would be interesting to know,' said John Cooper. 'One day he just took to limping. Whatever it is it's mighty trivial.'

He really is prejudiced, thought Linda. She finished her drink and went back to the stable flat where she settled down to write home.

'The weather is getting colder now,' she wrote, 'and there are great drifts of glowing leaves in the woods. I can see further from my window each day. Eventually, I fear, the new industrial estate being built over at Stoke Festing will be visible in the distance. Still, they're planting trees round the factories. You see what a country-lover your city daughter is becoming. I feel myself to be settling in here pretty well and acquiring useful knowledge of my patients. Doctor Cooper is always helpful and does not, I think, believe me to be a complete fool. But his son, though he likes me personally, is not convinced! This may bring him into the partnership quicker than all his father's entreaties. But not too soon, I hope, or all my careful spadework will be wasted.'

And I *have* worked hard, thought Linda, as she prepared for bed. I really have tried to understand the lives of these country folk and to get to know them really well so that they'll trust me as they do Doctor Cooper.

Three weeks passed and Bill Mullett's mother-in-law had just got over her bout of bronchitis, when Linda was called to her again. She'd sprained her ankle it seemed.

'How long have you been in this pain?' asked Linda.

'Only a day or two,' said the woman, wincing as she was touched. 'I didn't want to bother anyone.'

'You should have got them to call me before,' said Linda. 'I can certainly ease it a little for you.'

Mrs Piggot smiled gratefully.

'How did you do it?'

'Well. Promise you won't tell Bill and Muriel, because I wouldn't want to upset them, but I fell off a chair while I was dusting the top of the wardrobe.'

'It wasn't necessary for you to do that surely?' said Linda crossly. 'Especially so soon after being ill.'

'But they were so busy and I do like to help out about the place.'

'Well they shouldn't have let you. Now you'd better keep the leg rested for a day or two.'

'Oh dear, what a nuisance I'm going to be to them,' said Mrs Piggot anxiously. 'And they've so much to do just now.'

Poor old thing, thought Linda, and felt quite hostile towards the Mulletts, who would seem to be getting rather over-preoccupied with their new business.

At the door Linda met Miss Andrews collecting more sewing from Mrs Mullett. 'Although I haven't finished the first lot yet,' admitted the seamstress guiltily.

'Hold on, I'll give you a lift home,' said Linda, and turned back to Muriel Mullett.

'Your mother has pulled a ligament quite severely, please make sure she rests it.' Linda spoke firmly.

'I'll try to,' said the young woman, 'but Mum hates to be idle.'

That's a good excuse, thought Linda.

She guided Miss Andrews down the garden path and into the car. And 'guided' was the term for both then and when she alighted at her house. Miss Andrews seemed inclined to need direction, and twice she stumbled quite badly and had to be supported. But she assured Linda she felt perfectly well and waved her off with a cheerful smile.

Two more weeks passed before Linda, returning from a call, found the BMW in the yard. Why hadn't Peter telephoned in all this time? I'll ask them *both* over for supper tonight, she thought, and sent a message across via Elsie Peach to this effect, and received back word of acceptance.

The decision was impulsive and the fridge looked alarmingly empty. Linda grabbed a basket and set off for the village shops at a brisk trot. As she passed through the gate she caught sight of Peter hanging out of a top window, chatting with Bill Mullett who had graduated to the high guttering.

The butcher obliged her with a fine piece of pork and she packed it round with apples, onions and thyme and popped it in the oven. She knew old Doctor Cooper had a weakness for creamed potatoes so she prepared those and the fresh beans Elsie had brought from her garden. The village grocer had offered to bring up a block of ice-cream after he closed and Linda knew a recipe for butterscotch sauce that she herself had broken many a diet for.

Her kitchen was very small and towards zero hour seemed stacked from floor to ceiling with used saucepans. Linda pushed them into a corner, draped a tea towel over them and dived for the bathroom. Fifteen minutes later she was welcoming in the Coopers, looking cool and elegant in cream crepe with copper bangles – and only one fingernail smudged – which was pretty good going.

The two men were gratifyingly complimentary on the meal and Peter kept them amused by his adventures in New York. As the father and son threw back their heads in laughter, Linda thought again how alike they were and was aware of the warm surge of affection she felt for both.

Taking the opportunity to follow her into the kitchen carrying empty plates, Peter shut the door behind him and kissed her lightly on the neck.

'I've been looking forward to seeing you again. Have you missed me?'

'Yes I have,' said Linda, honestly.

'It's been wild at the hospital. I've only slipped down now for a vital chat with the old man. And I've a stack of people I have to see locally.'

Linda forced a smile on to her face. 'Well – so long as you're flourishing. And I can see you are.'

She led the way out of the room with the next course. She felt unsure of herself and disappointed that Peter was apparently not going to allot her any of his time on this visit.

The conversation turned to the new decorations to the surgery. Peter approved of the colours.

'And now the rest of the house must be done,' said John Cooper. 'This job alone should get Bill Mullett well started on the road to success, if it breaks me in the process!'

'He and his wife are certainly throwing their back into things,' said Peter. 'I had a chat to him. I think he'll do well.'

'Yes,' said Linda. 'As long as he doesn't kill his mother-in-law in the process. I suspect she's getting rather put upon. They're very lucky to have her running the house and coping with the child so that they can be free to operate the business, you know. After all, she's brought up one family and might expect to sit back a bit. But she's obviously completely devoted to them and utterly unselfish.'

'She sounds rather tiresome,' said Peter, making a joke.

But Linda flushed with irritation.

Even though he hung back at the door to whisper to her that she looked lovely, Linda felt unable to respond. Maybe she had read too much into his light flirtation.

Earlier on, Doctor Cooper had given her the hint that his son took full advantage of his attractions for the opposite sex. She was probably one of a number of conquests. Conquest? There hadn't been one in the fullest sense and she was glad everything had been light-hearted.

She must view it as something pleasant that had helped to speed her recovery from the blues and take an interest in life again. And Peter had certainly done that.

She must keep control. Enjoy Peter's delightful company whenever it was on offer. If he wanted it all to be superficial then that's how they'd play it. Maybe he wasn't a person who had very deep feelings anyway. She remembered his remark at table. Hadn't that been pretty cynical?

But she had cause to reflect on this again when a conversation with Bill Mullett the very next day threw fresh light on his domestic scene.

The young man looked thoroughly fed-up and glad to let off steam to someone.

'My mother-in-law took a pile of accounts with her to post and lost the lot on the bus. She was on her way to physiotherapy. She *would* take them, thinking she'd save me time. And she *would* take the bus though I wanted to run her in by car. Twice she got stuck at the bus stop in the rain and now she tells me this morning she left all my accounts on the bus last week. She didn't tell me before in case it worried me! She was hoping someone would find them and post them. Well they didn't!'

Linda suddenly saw another aspect to selfless devotion.

''Course she'd do anything in the world for us, you know,' he said. 'She's a wonderful person.' And his eye twitched violently. 'We can't hurt her feelings.'

That's the trouble, thought Linda. Two good-natured people being smothered with love by a third! It annoyed Linda to think she had jumped so readily to conclusions about the situation. But she was even more disturbed by a piece of news that Bill Mullett let forth before he went. It seemed that the sewing given to Miss Andrews had not been heard of since and when they had called to ask after it, Stuart Andrews had answered the door and their enquiries unsatisfactorily and with rudeness. Nothing had been seen of Miss Andrews for some time.

Linda was in a quandary. She felt troubled, but as she

had received no call to attend, could do nothing officially. Perhaps Miss Andrews had gone away for a while.

The matter went out of Linda's mind until surgery when Stuart Andrews limped in to see her and asked for a bottle of tonic for his sister.

'She's run down, I imagine. She doesn't seem to want to get up,' he said resentfully.

'I'll come and see her as soon as I've finished surgery.'

'That's not necessary. Just a bottle of tonic –'

'How will I know what to put in it, unless I know what's pulling her down?' asked Linda, with commendable patience.

He agreed reluctantly. Linda had the feeling he wouldn't have come at all if there'd been anyone else to get his meals.

She got a shock when she saw Mary Andrews. The woman was clearly very ill. Her skin hung yellow and loose over her bones and her eyes were sunk in dark shadows. She smiled, but so wearily that Linda felt an instinctive pang. At last, in response to Linda's questions she admitted she had been in pain for some time.

'Why didn't you come to see me?' asked Linda, almost angrily. But she knew the reason.

Linda spoke to Stuart Andrews. 'Your sister will have to go to hospital.'

'How long for?' queried Stuart irritably.

'Mr Andrews,' said Linda, 'your sister is extremely ill. Weren't you aware she was deteriorating like this?'

The man didn't answer, and Linda went on.

'I do not know how long she will be in hospital. It is almost certain she will need an operation and I want you to understand that I am gravely concerned about her.'

Somehow she had to impress on this self-centred man that his sister's condition was serious.

Her words had some effect for he looked suddenly alarmed and when he spoke his voice had lost some of its self-pitying whine.

He began asking questions, mostly concerned with the running of the house in Mary's absence.

Patiently his sister acquainted him with the necessary details.

Meantime, Linda went next door to telephone for an ambulance and when she returned Stuart was busy in the study and Miss Andrews alone in her room. She beckoned Linda close and indicated that she should shut the door.

'Would you do something for me, Doctor? Telephone the solicitors and ask them to come and see me. I've never made a Will you see, and I think I should.'

Linda did not argue.

'Certainly,' she said briskly, 'that'll be no trouble.'

'I want to leave him the house. I want there to be no mistake this time. It must be legal. I offered to give it to him in the past you know, but he'd never hear of it.'

Linda telephoned the firm of solicitors when she got back to surgery, then she sought out Doctor Cooper. She knew he would be upset by the news about Miss Andrews but she was unprepared for Peter's reaction.

She found the two men at lunch. Linda had not exaggerated her concern about Mary Andrews, and she told John Cooper her fears. He rose from the table, grim-faced, and left the room without a word.

His son watched him go, then turned on Linda.

'Why was she allowed to get to this state?'

'I was never called before.'

'Surely you had some indication she was ill. In a village as small as this –'

'Yes, I did suspect at one time, but how could I know? And anyway I couldn't barge in if I wasn't sent for.'

'There are ways of doing these things, you know that! If she had been my father's patient – neither he nor the old partner have ever bothered over much with the niceties of etiquette. They just saw when they were needed.'

Linda fully realised his words were prompted by a personal anguish about Miss Andrews, but she was still stung by what she considered was their injustice.

'I quite realise I've a lot to learn as a General Practitioner, Peter, but the sort of intuition you mean surely comes from long acquaintance with people, and don't forget I've not been here that long! And wasn't it you who warned me about interfering when I wasn't wanted.'

'That was in personal matters – not medical ones!'

'I'm quite prepared to believe you'd make a better job of it here than me, because you already know a lot of the locals personally – but for no other reason! But when you do join your father, you may have to re-think your idea of a simple country doctor with a finger on everybody's pulse. This Practice is growing. That new industrial estate is already affecting things. It'll not be all as you imagine it!'

Linda walked out.

She felt very badly about Miss Andrews and to have it implied that she might have in some way neglected her duty was painful.

Soon afterwards, she overheard Peter arranging to send flowers to Miss Andrews and realised he and his father knew and cared for her more than she'd appreciated.

So when Peter sought her out and offered her an apology for his words, she accepted it at once and offered him her own.

'Let's have a drink together before I have to go back to London.'

'I'd like that, Peter.'

They drove out to a little pub and sat cosily in a corner, enjoying each other's company as before. And later they took a lingering farewell in Linda's flat – and discovered more about each other. Linda felt happy and at ease again.

Peter rose to leave at last.

'I'll be seeing you!' he said, ruffling her hair.

'When?' Despite all her good intentions the word came out.

'Not sure. I'm going skiing.'

Linda instantly had a vision of long-limbed Nursing Sisters, in elegant ski-gear, skilfully descending the sun-kissed snow-slopes in hot pursuit of Peter; or snuggled up in chummy groups by log-fires quaffing gluwein.

'I'm in a racing team,' he added, as if reading her thoughts.

The vision changed immediately to a horrifying high ski-jump with Peter hurtling down it, hitting a hidden rock, turning a somersault, limbs twisted, broken …

'Take care of yourself,' said Linda, anxiously.

'Thank you for that. I will.'

Miss Andrews had her operation, but the surgeon made no bones about the fact that he considered he had been called too late.

When Linda drove in to the hospital a day or two later John Cooper asked to go with her as he wanted to visit his friend personally.

On the journey he told Linda more of Mary Andrews' history. Her mother had brought her up to believe that her brother was someone special, so that when the old lady died Mary did not question that she should go on attending to the wants of this indulged man. He had never done a hand's turn of work and they had scraped along on a tiny allowance he had and what money Mary could earn by sewing for friends and neighbours.

'She sacrificed her life entirely to that wretched man,' finished John Cooper, 'and she was a sweet girl, and turned down several offers of marriage.'

He lapsed into silence and Linda realised that John Cooper's must have been one of them. He didn't speak again but spent the rest of the drive lost in thought.

The Ward Sister informed them that Miss Andrews was comfortable and that her solicitor was at the moment with her, so they waited and were fortified with mugs of tea that reminded Linda sharply of the hospital days that seemed far behind her now.

Soon the solicitor came out of the little side ward and joined them. He looked perplexed.

'Excuse me, Sister,' he said. 'But I'm afraid Miss Andrews must be a little delirious.'

'I don't think so,' said the startled Sister. 'Weak perhaps, but she was certainly all right just now.'

'Well she speaks plainly enough, but it's very curious, she's trying to bequeath the house to her brother.'

'But that's right,' interjected Linda. 'I know she wants to do so very much.'

The solicitor frowned. 'But she must surely know,' he said. 'That house has been the property of her brother since their mother died nearly forty years ago.'

The two doctors stared at each other, both understanding very well what Stuart Andrews had done.

By pretending the house had been left to her instead of him as promised, he had laden her with such a sense of obligation and guilt that he had gained himself a lifelong slave.

When Linda went in to see Miss Andrews she knew at once that the woman also knew the truth at last. Her eyes had an expression of pain, but there was still no bitterness, and even now she tried to find excuses for her brother's cruelty.

'He was so frightened of being left alone,' she

whispered. 'He was always afraid of being alone.' She sighed: 'What will he do now?'

John Cooper stayed behind with Miss Andrews when Linda left, saying he would get a taxi later.

They both knew it was unlikely Miss Andrews would recover and Linda undertook to have a word with Stuart Andrews to prepare him.

That Doctor Cooper thought the man a monster, she knew, but as she drove swiftly back towards Stoke Dabenham, Linda found herself considering what motives could make a person bind another to them in such a way. What desperate fear of loneliness? Or had it been some unrecognised attachment to Mary herself. Had it been the fear of losing her, she having perhaps taken his mother's place in his mind, that caused him to secure her to him with such subtle cunning. Either way it was the result of such deep-seated need that Linda felt it possible to pity the man.

She reached the village and drew up outside the Andrews' house. She noticed the ledges of the panels and fluted moulding round the door were dusty, and the dolphin no longer shone.

At last her knocking was answered.

Stuart Andrews opened the door and Linda stepped into the hall. She could see through into Mary Andrews' sewing room and noticed a figure there busy with string and brown paper. It was Mrs Piggot. She looked up and nodded at Linda.

'Good afternoon, Doctor. I'm just collecting up Muriel's loose covers. Poor Miss Andrews never got them done. I suppose I'll have to do them now.'

'I've just come from the hospital, Mr Andrews,' said Linda.

'How is she?' asked Stuart Andrews. 'I shall try to get in to see her this evening.'

Linda turned and walked into the sitting room and he

followed; then had the grace to indicate that they should sit.

He listened silently as Linda explained considerately but positively the nature of Mary Andrews' illness and the possibility that she could not get better. She did not dwell on the fact of matters having all been left too late since it could not help. Her purpose now was to soften a blow which was to be almost a certainty.

Stuart Andrews took in the information gravely. He looked quite desolate. Finally he spoke.

'But what will I do?'

Linda looked into the moist self-pitying eyes and all the compassion drained out of her.

She rose.

He trailed her into the hall, all the while talking on about how difficult it was going to be for him to run the house by himself, how expensive it was to have any maintenance done on a place of that nature, and the impossibility of him tackling the everyday domestic matters of cleaning and cooking, to which he had never been accustomed or had any experience.

Mrs Piggot emerged from the sewing room with her load of material and stood wide-eyed as she listened to Andrews pouring out his troubles.

Linda saw her face suffused with a warm glow of interest at the prospect of this completely dependent human being in such desperate need of unlimited attention.

'Oh, Mr Andrews,' she said sympathetically, 'if there's any little thing I can do for you.'

Linda left them deep in earnest conversation. She drove quietly through the village, through the gates of the big house and round to the yard.

Perhaps out of this sorrowful business one tiny advantage might come. If Mrs Piggot devoted some of her well-intentioned energies towards Stuart Andrews' welfare, it might relieve the weight on the Mulletts' backs a bit.

Linda lit the fire in her flat and sat down in front of it, thinking of Mary Andrews and the circumstance that had ordered the pattern of her life.

Much later she heard John Cooper arrive back. She looked from the window. A friend had brought him home and was parking down in the yard.

She saw the two men get out of the car and go in through the back entrance of the big house. The doctor turned under the light and as he shut the glass door, Linda saw his shoulders stooped in an attitude of grief.

CHAPTER SIX

A WOMAN OF PARTS

As Linda stepped into the bath for the second time the telephone rang again. Wrapping the damp towel round herself once more she hurried to answer it.

It was Mrs Perry from the surgery. 'Doctor Ford?'

Who else, thought Linda.

'I'm sorry to bother you again, but another call has just come through. From Yelchester Hall – the Boys' School, you know.'

Linda adjusted the towel and took up a pencil.

'All right, Mrs Perry, I'm taking a note.'

'Mrs Beale, one of the housemasters' wives, was asking whether Doctor Cooper was going to call today to see her husband.'

'Did you tell her Doctor Cooper was away?'

'Yes.'

'What's wrong with Mr Beale?'

'He's recovering from a pneumothorax, Doctor.'

'I see. All right, I'll call in later on. Thank you, Mrs Perry.'

Linda trailed back to the bathroom. Her fragrant bubble bath lay before her chilled and scummy. She gave it best, towelled herself briskly dry and consoled herself by putting on her new suit.

John Cooper was the school doctor for Yelchester Hall, and Linda had never had occasion to pay it a call herself. Now she turned the M.G. in at the high gates and looked about for directions. Mrs Perry had said that the Beales were in Feldon House.

She stopped a small boy and he pointed out a red brick building across the quadrangle. As Linda drew up, four more boys in regulation flannel converged on the car and began examining it with critical interest.

In the hall, Linda hesitated, caught like a signpost at a crossroads of bustling students. Somewhere a bell was ringing. Purposeful figures in varying sizes hurried past, down passages and through doors and away. Suddenly the hall was deserted and Linda began looking about for some means of making her presence known. I'd better not ring a bell, she thought, or they'll all pop out again.

Then a young man appeared wearing an academic gown, caught sight of her, and came forward smiling. He had a handsome, sensitive face and he regarded Linda with interest.

'I'm Henderson,' he said, 'can I help you?'

He's not much older than his charges, thought Linda. She explained that she was temporarily in place of Doctor Cooper and he led the way upstairs with a sideways look that indicated plainly he thought the substitution a nice change.

As they reached the landing, a woman came out of one of the doors. She was pretty with soft brown hair piled romantically on top of her head, and wisps escaping about her face. When she saw them she stopped and frowned at Henderson.

Very quickly, the young man introduced Linda.

'The doctor?' said the woman in some surprise, but her brow at once cleared and she came forward with a welcoming smile.

'I'm Mrs Beale. Do come through to the study.'

With a single, warm look back at Henderson, she led the way down a corridor.

Linda followed her and Henderson leapt away downstairs to his duties.

Mrs Beale showed Linda into a dark panelled room and graciously presented her husband, who was sitting in a winged armchair with a rug wrapped round his knees.

Henry Beale was some years older than his wife, who fluttered round him adjusting cushions at his back, an attention he obviously found irritating for he pushed her hands away and suggested she should leave the room in a tone of voice that was barely polite.

Mrs Beale planted a fond kiss on his brow and floated away, having opened the neck of his shirt.

The Housemaster was making a good recovery but being a man deeply involved in his work he was impatient with his enforced idleness. He was desperately keen to take up full control of his House again and escape from the well-meant care of his wife which he did not hesitate to announce he found unendurable.

Linda was able to cheer him by the news that he would probably be active in a very short while, and the examination being at end, he rang a bell. Mrs Beale at once appeared, to accompany Linda out. She seemed overjoyed at the prospect of her husband being back to normal before long, and Linda hastened to warn her that Mr Beale's condition still called for great care as the lungs were very vulnerable.

'Don't worry, Doctor,' said Mrs Beale earnestly, 'he won't be allowed to do anything foolish.' She frowned. 'Somehow I'll stop him. Oh, by the way, while you're here, Doctor,' she added, 'would you just take a look at young Jilkes. He came out in a rash this morning. I think it's –' She faltered, losing confidence. 'Well, I'm not sure.'

'Where is he?'

'Matron's put him in the Sanatorium. I'll get a chap to take you over.'

Linda attended the mildly-measled little boy and afterwards was just climbing into her car when she realised she had left her gloves in Feldon House. She ran back up the steps into the hall, then remembered they were upstairs on a landing table.

There was no sign of anyone about, but just as she was gathering them up she heard Mrs Beale speaking from behind a door nearby, and what she said riveted Linda to the spot.

'Oh God, Paul, he's getting better! Everything will be back to normal!'

It was said in such anguished tones that Linda half expected to hear it followed by sobs. Instead there came a second voice, equally tortured.

'Oh, my dear!' it said sympathetically.

Linda tiptoed downstairs hastily, taking every precaution not to be seen, for the second voice was Henderson's.

Lord, thought Linda as she drove off, I nearly stumbled on a touching scene then.

That evening, Doctor Cooper telephoned and spoke to Linda. She assured him that she was managing quite satisfactorily during his brief visit to a sick friend, and was gratified when he did not sound excessively surprised or relieved. John Cooper had the gift of making her feel capable and trusted and this gave her self-confidence. She took the opportunity to discuss with him matters concerning one or two of their patients. Henry Beale's case was amongst them, and she couldn't help introducing Mrs Beale into the conversation with an oblique reference. John Cooper took it up.

'Is she coping?' he enquired. 'She was distraught when her husband went into hospital. I thought I was going to have a breakdown on my hands as well. Then she started haunting the wards and bestowing gifts of flowers and chocolates on all the staff. The nurses nicknamed her Lady Bountiful because of the way she gushed all over them.'

'How funny,' said Linda, 'yet Mrs Perry says when Mrs Beale phones her about the boys, she's completely business-like, in fact quite tough and demanding.'

'She's quite a chameleon – changing her character to suit the occasion.'

'Certainly a woman of parts,' said Linda.

'All things to all men,' chuckled John Cooper, as he rang off.

He could be right there, thought Linda, as she put her gloves away, remembering the whispers behind the door.

She got out a thicker pair and collected her Wellington boots. There was a call to be made to a farm cottage, and Linda knew the road up to it was flooded and she'd be picking her way over the fields. Two days ago she'd left part of her skirt decorating the barbed wire fence.

It was raining as she set off, so she borrowed an old deerstalker hat she found on the surgery hall-stand. Desperate situations call for desperate measures, she told Mrs Perry, cheerfully.

The receptionist laughed. After their uneasy start, the two women had found they worked together well, and Linda was grateful for Mrs Perry's efficient organisation without which she could never have handled John Cooper's work as well as her own for these few days.

When Linda next called to see Jilkes at Yelchester Hall, she found her own way to the Sanatorium. Again, as she left her car, a group of small boys attached themselves to it, discussing its merits. Linda smiled warmly. She was rather devoted to her little treasure.

Jilkes was sitting up in bed reading *The Farmer and Stock Breeder*. Linda glanced at Matron with amused surprise.

'Jilkes' father raises pedigree Jersey cows,' explained Matron, adding wryly, 'as I am now well aware.'

Jilkes grinned.

'I shall not be sorry when he's better, Doctor. He has told me more about the pedigree Jersey cow than I wish to know.'

Linda sat down on Jilkes' bed. 'We've got something in common then,' she said to the boy. 'My father owns a dairy and milk-round.'

'Does he?' said Jilkes, clearly astonished to find that doctors had fathers, let alone dairies.

'Yes,' ventured Linda, 'he's a sort of dairy Godfather.'

Jilkes fell about with mirth.

Matron went off to make Linda a cup of coffee, while the little boy told her all about the prize herd which was the pride of his family, and Linda told him about the old-fashioned shop in the East End of London that had been her home as a child; with its tiled walls and counter, and the yard at the back for the milk floats.

As she spoke Linda felt a pang of nostalgia. She could smell again the fresh cream, the cheese and the gammon ham. She remembered her mother's clean-scrubbed rosy arms emerging from her spotless overall. The shop had always been a cool oasis in its dingy setting. It had had its day, of course, and even now Linda knew there were moves afoot for it to be taken over by a large combine, together with several neighbouring shops, to make a big, new supermarket. Her father had written about the matter only a few days ago. She was glad he didn't seem upset.

Later, Linda left young Jilkes busy impressing the Matron with an account of record milk yields. She made her way across the quadrangle towards Feldon House, to look in on Henry Beale.

Mounting the stairs through a cascade of students, she went along towards the study. She knocked lightly. There was no reply so Linda opened the door and peered in.

Oh dear, she thought, I've done it again. For across the room in an alcove stood Mrs Beale, close folded in the arms of Paul Henderson. Evidently they had not heard her knock.

Mrs Beale recovered first. 'Oh good morning, Doctor Ford,' she said brightly, and came forward patting back a stray hair. 'My husband's not properly up yet. I'll just find out if he's fit to be seen.' She darted off.

Henderson and Linda stood for a moment in silence each looking at separate walls of the room. Then the young man spoke.

'I – I think I ought to explain.'

'You don't have to,' said Linda, 'it's none of my business.'

'But I'd like to.'

He seemed very agitated and it was not just embarrassment.

'Very well.' Linda sat down and listened.

'Mrs Beale is desperately unhappy,' he began. 'You can't imagine what a life she has with that man. He's utterly inconsiderate. Half the time you'd think she just didn't exist and the other half he finds some pretext on which to bully and harass her until she's completely demoralised. I've tried to give her what small comfort I can but she's nearly at her wit's end!'

And so are you, thought Linda, looking into his strained face.

'I'll confess she's come to mean a very great deal to

me,' he went on, 'and I just can't bear to stand by and watch her suffer! What can one do? Somehow she must be helped. He must be made to stop tormenting her. She's too gentle, Doctor. She has no weapons against him. Can you do anything? Is there nothing you could say to him?'

Linda looked dubious. Henderson turned away in despair. She laid a hand on his arm.

'I'll see if the opportunity presents itself,' she offered. 'But you know, unless one knows the full circumstances –'

It was not feasible, she knew, but she could also see that the woman had become the young schoolmaster's fairy princess, and that he saw it his duty to slay her dragon-husband. Another role for the lady and she seemed to be playing it well.

'He's a bloody monster!' said Paul Henderson. His voice broke on the last word and he hurried from the room with his head down.

A few moments later Mrs Beale came back and collected Linda to take her to her husband's bedroom as he was still not up. She was perfectly composed and took her place by his pillow, laying her hand on his shoulder fondly.

'It's all right, Doctor,' said Beale. 'I'm not feeling bad. Just had a lot of mail this morning. I must say, though, I'm getting mighty bored sitting about.'

'You must do as the doctor says, Henry dear,' said Mrs Beale, shaking her head at him in affectionate reproach. She began to pick up some of the envelopes scattered over the bed.

'Leave them alone, you'll only muddle them up,' said Henry Beale testily.

'Well now,' said Linda, 'I had a word with Doctor Cooper about you. We think you should be fully active in two months. Does that cheer you up?'

'Two months. Splendid. That means I'll get a good run at the end of term. I've a good deal to clear up, you know.'

Mrs Beale looked up enquiringly.

'Yes,' said Linda. 'I imagine it's been difficult for you, having to leave things.'

'Not just that,' said Beale. 'I'm finishing here, you see. I've just heard this morning. I've got a Headship. A minor public school in the north.'

Linda was prevented from making the appropriate congratulations by Mrs Beale. Obviously the news was a complete surprise to her. She gave a gasp of dismay and quickly left the room.

Henry Beale gritted his teeth with annoyance.

'You must excuse my wife,' he said coldly. 'She lives in a dream world. I don't know why she chose to make a scene. It's a promotion, for heaven's sake. But then she always dramatises everything. She lives in a dream world,' he repeated.

'I wonder why,' said Linda pensively. It occurred to her that it was possibly because the woman felt shut out of the real one.

Henry Beale sighed. 'I should never have married such a young woman. It was a mistake. It's foolish of me to expect any better. One needs a really capable woman to partner one in a job like this.'

Linda wondered to what extent the man had ever given his wife a chance to develop in this respect. The many parts she adopted with such facility were perhaps all only substitutes for the true one in which her husband did not deem her fit to be cast.

'Heaven knows I demand little enough of her,' said Beale.

Too little perhaps, thought Linda. It could make a woman feel undervalued. She rose to go. She was a bit surprised that this man should have opened up as he had.

But Mrs Beale's reaction to the new job had created an opportunity for him to discuss their relationship, and Linda suspected he had welcomed it.

On the table by the door, Linda spotted a box of cigarettes lying in an opened gift-wrapping. She picked them up and carried them out of the room with her.

In the lounge she found Mrs Beale and handed her the box.

'If these were intended for Mr Beale, please make sure he does not smoke them at present. Cigarettes are strictly forbidden for the time being. They might cause a coughing spasm which could be extremely dangerous. Will you keep them away from him?'

'Oh, of course!' said Mrs Beale, taking the cigarettes. 'I'll put them right out of sight. I don't smoke myself. I know, I'll give them to Paul, then Henry just won't be able to find them. Henry's a very heavy smoker normally. He's really missing it, you know.'

'Well, you must impress on him that it is most unwise.'

Linda's drive home was a minor nightmare.

Something was wrong with the engine. Even as she started it, she knew there was some sort of trouble in the works. It was making a curious, stifled sound and there was no power worth speaking of in it. She limped out of the gates of Yelchester Hall under the eyes of the row of young motor-car fanciers. They'll have taken a few marks off this one now, thought Linda, ruefully.

She got less and less amused as she went on, however, for she could scarcely get the vehicle to go beyond ten miles an hour. Linda stopped and got out. She opened the bonnet and surveyed the engine suspiciously. The plugs were in place. Nothing looked loose or disconnected. She knew she had petrol. She got back in and drove on. But it was ludicrous going at this pace. She felt like a hearse.

There was no Garage between the school and Stoke Dabenham village, so she was obliged to continue her stately progress for the whole journey. At least I'm *going*, she thought, and hoped she wouldn't get a stream of traffic building up behind her. But it was a quiet country lane and she eventually reached home with only her own frayed nerves to contend with.

Mrs Perry greeted her with the news that the surgery appointments were particularly heavy and glanced rather pointedly at her watch. When she heard about the trouble with the car, however, she was immediately concerned to assist.

'I'll contact the Garage,' she said, 'and meantime there's Doctor Cooper's car, isn't there?'

Linda realised, with relief, that John Cooper had not driven to London. He had said he did not feel up to it and had gone by train. There was sure to be a key somewhere and he would certainly not mind her using it for the calls until the M.G. was back to normal.

When the last patient had finally been attended to, and the waiting room was empty, Linda wearily rose and went through into the sitting-room where Elsie Peach had prepared her a little supper. But the telephone rang almost at once and the matter was urgent.

'There!' said Elsie sympathetically. Then she quickly made up a sandwich of bread and cheese and thrust it in Linda's hand as she went out.

Linda knew it would give her hiccups but she was grateful for the kindness. It was certain she wasn't going to see a knife and fork again for a few hours.

Mrs Perry had been unsuccessful with the Garage which had already closed. She watched anxiously as Linda gave her car an experimental start. But it was still useless and she transferred to John Cooper's Rover. Mrs Perry climbed in beside her and Linda dropped her off at her house at the end of the village.

'Goodnight, Doctor Ford,' she said, and gave a tired smile.

Linda realised the last few days had been quite a strain for her as well.

'Doctor Cooper will be back tomorrow morning,' Linda reminded her, in the way of comfort. Then she sped on to deal with a young girl in Pretting who proved to require an immediate removal to hospital, for an appendix operation.

There were two other calls after this, which, although not emergencies, Linda deemed necessary in order that her patients should get comfortably through the night. One of them was to a house on the big estate which was being built as part of the new area of industrial development. Although the site was being well-planned and the factories and houses attractively laid out, it was not yet finished and so far had no character. All the buildings looked alike to Linda and with little lighting she soon found herself lost in a maze of unmade-up roads and half-built houses.

An hour later when she was at last pointing the Rover's nose towards home and bed, the moon was up and the back of her shoulders were stiff with fatigue. Never mind, she thought, her senior would be back to share the burden tomorrow.

Elsie Peach came out into the yard as she was parking the Rover. Linda's heart sank.

Another call?

'Doctor Cooper telephoned,' began Elsie.

'He *will* be back tomorrow?' asked Linda quickly.

'It wasn't Doctor Cooper who phoned, it was his son, Doctor Peter. Apparently his father had a bit of a bad turn this morning and he's driving him down here. Doctor Peter said it was not serious,' said Elsie, 'and you were not to wait up because he'll look after his father. I've got everything ready.'

'I see. Well, thank you, Elsie. But I really think I ought to.'

'Doctor Peter specially said for you to get your sleep, Doctor Ford, because Doctor Cooper won't be able to take surgery tomorrow morning and there's no point in you both being under the weather.'

That's sensible, agreed Linda. So although she felt far from happy about it, she took herself off to the stable flat and went to bed, where she was fast asleep long before Peter Cooper swung his car into the yard.

The next morning, Linda went across to the big house first thing. She found Peter having his breakfast. He waved to her to sit down and poured her a cup of coffee.

'The old boy's still in bed,' he said, 'but he says he'll be up for evening surgery – and knowing him I've no doubt he will.'

'What was wrong?'

'Nothing serious – if he's sensible. A very slight angina, we think. Too much booze with his old chum, probably.' He pointed the quip with a great swig at his cup.

Linda was not taken in by his flippancy. After all, he hadn't hesitated to drop everything and drive his father home.

'Anyway,' he continued cheerfully, 'he's got the message. He's got to ease off a bit. You can manage all right this morning, can't you?'

His tone was offhand and Linda realised that Peter had no conception of the number of patients the Practice now embraced; that he still thought of it as it had been when he was a child growing up in Stoke Dabenham when his father didn't even have the second surgery at Pretting. It's probably why he's so reluctant to come down here and be his father's partner, she thought. Because he imagines it's so dull! Well, when he *does* take over from me he'll find out it's a far cry from the well-ordered life and wide-spread responsibilities of hospital work.

She told him about the trouble she'd had with her car and he at once rose from the table and strode out to the yard to investigate, still carrying his coffee cup.

He switched on the ignition and revved up, making a face at what he heard. Then he gave his cup to Linda and flung up the bonnet. He frowned thoughtfully into the engine for a moment and then moved round the side of the car and sank out of view. A few seconds later he reappeared from round the back, with a puzzled look on his face.

'It doesn't seem to have any power,' said Linda.

'I'm not surprised,' said Peter. 'Your exhaust pipe's blocked.'

'Blocked?' queried Linda. 'Whatever with?'

'It looks like a currant bun.'

Linda remembered the row of innocent, boyish faces at Yelchester Hall.

Peter loosened the blockage with a screwdriver and at the next rev it flew out and the sound of the engine returned to normal.

Linda wondered whether she'd be able to recognise the culprits when next she called at the school and whether, if she did, she'd be able to reprimand them with a straight face.

Peter stayed on to lunch and all three doctors had it together. Elsie Peach served them rump steaks, whispering to Peter as she passed that she'd have got him his steak and kidney pudding if she'd had more time, but a pudding needed advance notice.

As she expected, Linda's morning had been very busy and she'd only had time to wash her hands and change her working shirt-blouse into a smarter one before the meal. But at least John Cooper seemed to be back on form again.

So Linda was slightly taken aback when Peter suddenly brought it into the conversation that he would be joining the Practice quite soon. Although she had known the day would come, Linda still found it a bit of a shock. She could see now that for all his casual manner, Peter was far from unobservant and had been keeping an eye on his father's health for some time.

'I'm fit as a flea!' protested John Cooper.

'Fitter, probably,' said Peter. 'But this has sort of brought things to a head.'

'I won't say I'll not be pleased to have you down here,' said his father, with a pat on Peter's arm.

'I've had my flat on the market for some time and at last there's a buyer interested. So I should think I'll come down by the end of the month.'

'That will suit very well, won't it, Linda?' said John Cooper.

'Oh, yes,' said Linda, her voice very businesslike. 'That will just fit in with the end of my contract.'

'Oh. Ah. Yes.' John Cooper sat back in his chair with a thoughtful frown.

Peter was calmly helping himself to more apple pie.

'What about your work at the hospital?' asked Linda.

'Oh, I finished up officially before I went sailing.'

'Oh, I see.'

'They've still been finding me plenty to do though. And I've had a few ends to tie up, of course.'

The two men chatted on, while Linda's thoughts roved. She must force her mind away from this Practice and towards a new appointment for herself. Tonight, in the flat, she'd do some serious thinking.

She was jerked back to conversation as John Cooper said: 'Is Susan's arm better now?'

'Oh yes, mending fine. Could have been worse. She would tear off down the Black Run. At the end of the day. Tired out. I warned her. But you know Susan.'

So it had been a mixed party, thought Linda. This 'Susan', whose name sometimes dropped so casually into the dialogue, had been part of it. Perhaps it had just been a party for two – Peter and Susan.

Why did it give her such a pang? Why did this talk of this other friend of Peter's, whom she had never met, and could not know whether they were close or not, make her feel alienated. Already, she felt herself withdrawing from this whole situation. The end of the month! Perhaps in another six months this would all be a memory – the Practice, the kindness of the old doctor, her friendship with Peter. Nothing but an experience to be remembered and put to good use.

Nevertheless, it had all meant a lot to her.

She looked up at Peter and found him eyeing her curiously. She smiled at him and he smiled back warmly. Whatever happened now she wouldn't have missed it for anything.

'Is your car all right now, Linda?' asked John Cooper.

'Good as new. Thanks to Peter. I'd never have suspected what it was.'

'And what was it?'

Peter told the story of the bun and John Cooper rocked with laughter.

'And I thought they were admiring it. Interested in M.G.s!'

'They probably were. I expect it was a sudden inspiration.'

'I don't think I'd better mention the matter to Mr Beale,' said Linda.

'I shouldn't if I were you – they'll probably get six of the best!' said Peter.

'In this case I think the punishment would probably fit the crime,' observed the doctor.

'Next time you visit Yelchester, give my love to Alice Beale,' remarked Peter, rising to leave.

Linda looked at him. He was wearing a mock-lecherous expression.

'Ha!' commented his father.

'She's not my father's favourite lady,' explained Peter, 'because she talks to him as if she's four years old. He's always afraid she's going to perch on his knee and gurgle. But it's different with me. She once got me in a dark cupboard and there was nothing childish about that!'

So for Peter she'd played the *femme fatale*, mused Linda. Certainly the lady suited herself to the occasion.

Linda next saw the Beales about ten days later. It was no more than a routine visit as Henry Beale was progressing well.

Paul Henderson was also in the room when Linda arrived. When he saw who it was he nodded politely to her and began to make his departure. He collected up some papers, which he and Henry Beale had obviously been discussing.

'Will you kindly see these are put away in the top drawer of my desk, Henderson?' said Beale. 'If they're left lying about here they're certain to get mislaid.'

It was a casual enough remark, but could be construed as a criticism of Mrs Beale. Linda shot her a look and observed that she had taken it as such.

She turned away from her husband and fixed Henderson with a meaning look, her eyes large with humiliation and pain.

Paul Henderson went white and carried the papers out of the room without a word.

Very soon Mrs Beale followed him out.

Henry Beale seemed unaware of any atmosphere and discussed his condition with Linda, expressing his usual impatience with it.

'How are the preparations going for your move?'

asked Linda, ready to scotch any rash plans her patient might have in mind.

'I'll deal with them as soon as I'm about.'

'You mustn't take on too much, you know.'

'Don't worry, I shall get a firm in, if I can find the right one.'

'Mrs Perry mentioned a good one the other day. Would you like me to get the name and phone your wife –'

Beale interrupted sharply. 'I shouldn't bother with Mrs Beale, she's not capable of handling this sort of organisation.' He sounded bitter. There was no doubt he believed his wife inadequate in practical matters, but Linda remembered Mrs Perry saying that the woman could be perfectly efficient when necessary.

'Mr Beale,' ventured Linda. 'Do you think it might be possible that you are underestimating your wife?'

'She play-acts at life,' he said, with perception.

'And you think the role of Headmaster's wife is out of her range?'

Henry Beale frowned. He became thoughtful. Very soon Linda took her leave.

'I've some pills for you in the car. I forgot them. I'll bring them up,' she said and went into the next room, where she found Henderson and Mrs Beale in intimate conversation.

Mrs Beale immediately broke off and accompanied Linda downstairs. Henderson stared after her for a moment then wheeled about and made for Beale's room.

In the hall, Mrs Beale was intercepted by a small boy and she remained listening to him whilst Linda collected the pills and returned upstairs to deliver them.

As she entered the room she was brought up short by the sight of Paul Henderson in the act of lighting a cigarette for Henry Beale.

'Stop!' Linda stepped over promptly and, removing the cigarette, threw it into the wastebasket. 'Mr Beale, I thought you understood that smoking was against orders. If you choose to ignore medical advice you will most certainly hamper your recovery and may well do yourself grave harm.'

She turned on her heel and went out to find Mrs Beale. Why do I always sound so pompous when I'm enraged, she thought. The schoolmasters had looked quite abashed. She found Mrs Beale coming upstairs.

Linda repeated her warning, angrily.

'Please let your friends know about this smoking rule,' she urged.

Mrs Beale looked dumbfounded. 'But Paul *did* know,' she said. 'I told him myself how dangerous it would be for Henry to smoke.'

The two women looked at each other, both realising that the young schoolmaster could only have done it with intent to harm.

At that moment Henderson appeared and Mrs Beale flew at him in fury. He stood rock-still in amazement as she accused him wildly of attempting to injure her husband – if not murder him. She burst into hysterical tears.

'But I did it for *you*,' he cried. He was staring at her in bewilderment. She shook her head. 'We love each other,' he said, catching her shoulders.

'You're mistaken,' she said.

'But he was a brute to you – a brute!'

'You're mistaken!'

They both stopped dead.

They've both been playing a game, thought Linda. A dangerous game – and now they both know it.

Henderson's hands fell from her and he walked off, without a backward glance.

Mrs Beale turned to Linda and brushed back her hair.

'Poor boy,' she said calmly. 'He must have been jealous of my husband's promotion.' And Linda could see that she had already begun to believe it. 'My husband is so dedicated and idealistic,' the woman went on, leading the way back upstairs. 'He's very vulnerable to the worldliness of lesser men.'

Finding the box of pills still in her hand, Linda followed her.

In Henry Beale's room she at once hurried across to his side and fluttered round him bestowing words of comfort and protection.

For once her husband did not brush her aside. Instead he was regarding her with speculation. He accepted without retort her admonishment about the smoking, submitted to having his legs tucked round with the rug and then brought up the subject of their move.

'Doctor Ford's offered to telephone through the name of a recommended removal firm,' he said. 'There'll be a great deal to do, Alice, and I'll need all your support.'

He's pondered my words, thought Linda, and is shrewd enough to be giving it a try. And he's lucky, because it'll fit in exactly with Mrs Beale's current portrayal.

Linda was right. Mrs Beale tweaked at her husband's cushions with authority.

'We'll get you well first, my dear, then tackle your new appointment together.' She looked up at Linda aglow. 'Heaven knows he needs taking care of,' she said.

'She's got her lead part at last,' remarked Linda to Doctor Cooper that evening, as they drank a late cup of tea together.

'Let's hope they have a long run.'

'It might work out,' said John Cooper, 'if he can continue to give her confidence in herself.'

'Not everybody has that special ability,' said Linda. She looked over at the older doctor gratefully. But he was gazing into the fire unaware.

CHAPTER SEVEN

TESTING TIMES

Her tyres screeched as Linda applied the brakes sharply at the STOP sign. She had not taken in fully the warning notice as she passed it. Fool! Her mind had been wandering. A driver wagged a finger at her and she ruefully pretended to shoot herself in the head. He shrugged. He's dismissing me as another stupid young woman driver, thought Linda. He'd probably give up if he knew I was meant to be a responsible doctor who's been in General Practice tending the sick populace for half a year.

Her six months contract was now at an end and she was actively seeking a new job. For the last three days she'd been in London for just this purpose, staying with her parents. And now she was speeding back to the West Country and would probably make it for evening surgery. She had not yet left for good, as Peter was still busy moving in. She pushed the problem of her future to the back of her mind and concentrated on the road.

Somewhere along the route, she knew, Peter was also

travelling. But she'd seen no sign of his BMW and had no idea whether he was ahead of or behind her.

She was held up a long time near Exeter and soon realised she was going to be much later than she had intended. She felt guilty. Surgery would probably be over by the time she arrived.

But it wasn't. The waiting room was still occupied by six people, four of them were her patients. They brightened as she entered. This surprised and pleased her. She was still modest enough to expect any of them to prefer the opportunity to see the senior doctor. But she was coming to find that some, particularly some of the younger women, quite favoured a woman doctor.

When the last patient had left, John Cooper came into her consulting room and invited her to take a glass of sherry with him. They went through to his lounge and sank into his deep winged chairs. She saw that he looked extremely tired.

'Another twelve patients registered while you were away,' he said.

'That must mean they've moved into those two new roads on the estate?'

He nodded.

Four more small factories had recently been erected and another was being finished in a valley a few miles south and gradually the employees were filling up the considerable complex of well-designed dwellings that had been built nearby for the purpose. It would soon be quite a township.

'I was intrigued by a certain patient of yours called Mrs Fenwick,' said John Cooper. 'She said you had told her to bring her baby for another visit. I must say I couldn't see anything in the least wrong with it myself, but perhaps it's made a miraculous recovery.'

He regarded Linda under his bushy eyebrows.

'You're right, of course, Doctor Cooper,' admitted

Linda. 'There's nothing wrong with the baby. It's the mother I'm bothered about. She moved on to the estate two months ago. I wondered very much when she kept bringing in a perfectly healthy baby and at last I got to the bottom of it. The girl's desperately lonely. She was coming simply for someone to talk to. Her husband's working long hours to get the new factory going and she's made no friends yet. She's come from a little street in a London suburb where she knew everyone and everything here is overwhelmingly strange.'

'Hm.' Doctor Cooper took a sip of sherry. 'Well, I understand what you were doing, of course, but I must say I found it a little irritating with a waiting room full of really sick cases.'

His tone was not censuring but Linda sensed a hint of criticism. It was a pity Sandra Fenwick had come that busy day. She hadn't normally taken up much time.

'Doctor Cooper,' began Linda, very earnestly, 'I really do consider it wise to keep an eye on Mrs Fenwick. She's in a rather nervous and depressed state.'

John Cooper gave a grunt and subsided. Linda wasn't sure whether he approved of her method but she knew he appreciated that she was in command of the situation.

'You didn't see my son Peter on the road?' he asked, turning to lighter matters.

'No.'

'I suppose he'll turn up at some ungodly hour. Well, I'll not be waiting up. He can scratch about in the fridge for his supper.'

Linda smiled. She knew well that Elsie Peach would have left ample provisions tucked away for Peter. She only hoped she'd remembered to leave a snack over in the stable flat for Linda to go back to. Elsie made a wonderful veal-and-ham pie and Linda wondered whether she might expect to find a portion of this allotted to her. Even if not, Elsie's sandwiches were in a class on their own; and maybe there'd be fruitcake ... Really she was feeling dreadfully hungry.

'Were your parents well?' enquired Doctor Cooper.

'Yes, thank you,' said Linda, finishing her sherry. 'We had a long talk about the dairy. It seems the Development Company is certainly going to buy them out. But the price has not yet been decided.'

'The day of the small man is over I sometimes think,' mused Cooper.

'It is in that part of London,' agreed Linda. 'Happily, Mum and Dad do not seem to mind at all. They've put in a good many years now and worked all hours with the milk round and the shop, I think they're looking forward to a rest.'

'That's good,' said the older doctor. 'A rest!' The word sparked off in him a gigantic yawn. 'Excuse me.'

Linda rose, then found herself overcome by a matching gape. They both laughed.

'Goodnight, Doctor Cooper.'

Linda crossed the yard of the big house and climbed hopefully up to the flat. There was a tray on the table with a white napkin protecting it. Linda lifted the corner. Elsie had turned up trumps again.

I'm going to be sorry to leave this place for a good many reasons, reflected Linda. She had, of course, omitted to mention to John Cooper the subject that had dominated her parents' conversation – their daughter's next post. In this respect her trip to London had been unproductive.

Some time during the night Peter eventually arrived and there was a message from him on her desk when Linda went over to her consulting room to take morning surgery. It read: 'Some friends of mine are giving a party at Whitring tonight. They'd like you to come. Are you free? The atrocities begin at nine!'

Linda telephoned through on the extension and got

Elsie who went in search of Peter. A few minutes later his sleepy voice came through.

'You got me up,' he said.

'Sorry. But I'll be up to my eyes in a minute. About the party. I'd love to come but I've surgery here and a stack of calls to make.'

'Come late.'

'I'll try.'

'I'll come back and collect you.'

'No don't. Give me the address and I'll do my best to get there. It would be fun.'

'Of course it would. You can't work all the time.'

'You should see our appointments list!'

Linda rang off. Wait till you're in my seat, she thought.

It was true, as Mrs Perry confirmed when she brought in an armful of dossiers.

'You'll be going out to Pretting later, will you Doctor Ford?' said Mrs Perry.

'Yes,' said Linda, remembering that she also had a two-hour stint to do at the little outpost surgery.

'There you are then,' said Mrs Perry, and passed over another batch of records. 'I hope you had a nice trip to London, but we're certainly glad you're back!' She smiled suddenly before whisking out of the room.

She should do that more often, thought Linda. It makes her look quite pretty.

Linda flexed her shoulder-blades purposefully. Then she stretched out a finger and buzzed for the first patient.

It was a hard day and when she looked in her mirror at nine-thirty that evening, her heart sank. She was not at all sure she had the energy to do the great paint job that was called for.

Then the telephone rang.

'Are you sagging?' It was Peter's voice.

'Well – yes.'

'Come on in – the water's fine!'

Linda could hear music in the background. That did it. She loved to dance.

'I'll be right there!' she cried.

She started for the bathroom. Catching sight of her reflection in the mirror, she stopped in surprise. She grinned at herself. Confucius he say, excitement is the best face pack!

She was gratified by the impression made by her entrance. Peter introduced her widely and had cornered her some supper, but thereafter she had to share him with several good-looking girls who seemed to know him quite intimately. But she herself was much in demand, and when the party broke up Peter was there beside her announcing that he intended to drive home behind her and see she arrived home safely.

'But do go slowly,' he pleaded, 'I'm tired.'

He was tired!

It was a sharply clear night, with a bright moon illuminating the quiet countryside. By the time they turned into the yard, both had fallen under the spell of the moment. They closed their car doors quietly and moved to each other. They kissed, then stood wrapped in each other's arms, the frost forming on their intermingled breath.

Linda felt suspended in time. How nice if this single moment could go on and on. But nothing in life remains the same – not for a solitary second. And what a comfort that thought can be at times! Nevertheless ...

'I'll be sorry to finish here at the end of the week,' she said.

'End of the week?' said Peter.

'I hope you'll find General Practice – fulfilling,' she hurried on. 'I hope you'll be as happy here as I've been.'

'You don't need to move out of the flat, of course,' said Peter. 'I'll be living in the house.'

'Thanks –'

'You could stay till you land something you really fancy.'

'I don't think so,' said Linda. And left it at that.

If she tried to explain how she would hate to be living nearby yet not working as a doctor in that little community, Peter might not understand. Might see it as emotional involvement again. And she could never put into words what she felt about Peter himself. He had said that after she left they would keep in touch and maybe they would, but she knew nothing was going to be the same. Somehow the Practice, John Cooper and Peter were all intertwined for her.

She suddenly felt dreadfully tired.

'I'm exhausted,' she said.

Peter nuzzled her cheek, and slipping his arm round her waist he supported her gently to her door, where he drew off her glove and kissed the palm of her hand.

'Nothing's going to change,' he said.

'No, of course not,' answered Linda.

He doesn't understand, she thought. When all my books and belongings have been removed and his have taken their place and I drive away it will be as if I was never here. He will take his rightful place beside his father and everyone will forget I ever came to Stoke Dabenham.

Peter opened the door for her but didn't make to follow. They wished each other goodnight quietly and easily and went their separate ways in silence.

Linda would have dearly loved to have slept late next morning, but she was summoned to one of her patients at seven o'clock. When she returned, John Cooper called her in for a coffee. He and Peter were at breakfast. It seemed the older doctor had been called out three times during the night.

'This Practice is getting out of hand since the new estate was begun. And there are a lot more people to move in yet.' John Cooper turned to his son. 'I think we've got to the stage where it could support a third partner.'

Linda set down her cup and listened closely.

The two men were only talking casually, but they weighed the situation up and in the end both seemed to be in agreement that the rapidly increasing numbers on their register justified three doctors.

How wonderful, thought Linda, if I could just stay on when Peter joins the partnership! How, she wondered, would her bank manager react. There would be equipment to buy and – her speculations were stopped short by Peter's next words.

'I think Tom Doyle would be interested in coming in with us,' he remarked.

Before John Cooper could offer an opinion the telephone rang and he became engaged in conversation with the anxious parents of a sick child.

Linda and Peter rose. He was off to the County Health Office. She made her way back to the stable flat, where she slumped down in an armchair. Disappointment engulfed her.

Why had she imagined they would offer her a partnership? Yet why not? Perhaps John Cooper suspected she had no capital available. She'd never made a secret of her background. But then it had been Peter who had jumped in so quickly with the suggestion of Tom Doyle – whoever he might be. One of Peter's colleagues at the hospital, Linda suspected.

Neither of the men had thought immediately of her. Maybe she'd not fitted in as well as she'd thought. She began trying to remember where she could have fallen short in her duty or crossed John Cooper with an opposing attitude.

Stop it, she said to herself sharply, that way madness lies. You've done six month's solid work here to the best of your ability. That's all you were engaged for and now it's coming to an end. And that's all there is to it.

Nevertheless, as she tidied her cosy little lounge she smoothed the chintz covers with affection.

As she neatened the curtains she looked from the window and across the rolling fields. A pale sun glittered on the last of the melting frost.

She telephoned to thank her hostess for the party and was warmed by the friendly response.

It's no use, thought Linda, I shall miss this place. It's strange that you can live your whole life in the city and yet so quickly feel part of the countryside.

Linda found herself using words to this effect as a form of comfort for Mrs Fenwick, when, to Linda's dismay, she turned up at surgery again. But this time at least she made no pretence that it was on behalf of the baby, which was jiggling happily on her lap.

'My husband thinks I'm run down and need a tonic,' she said.

'Yes,' said Linda, 'how's your appetite?'

'All right.'

'Are you sleeping well?'

'Yes.'

Then suddenly the girl's composure forsook her. Her eyes filled with tears and she drew in a great shuddering breath.

'Oh, Doctor, I'm not run down!' she burst out. 'I just hate it here!'

'You're still lonely?' said Linda gently.

'I don't know anybody and I never seem to see anybody and there's nowhere to go and nothing to do –' She was crying miserably.

The baby put up its starfish hands and dabbled them on her cheeks.

Linda was glad she had cried at last. It would relieve tension.

'And Blackie got caught in a snare and had to be put to sleep. I hate the countryside!'

'That was unfortunate,' said Linda, with genuine sympathy.

'You're from the town, Doctor, you understand.'

Linda understood very well how alien her new surroundings seemed to Sandra Fenwick. She remembered how many surprises she'd had herself. She'd expected it to be quiet. Instead there was always something to be heard – dogs, sheep, birds, aeroplanes, tractors, howling wind! She'd expected common land to take walks on, and was surprised to discover that every inch of soil seemed to belong to somebody and you passed over it as a favour.

Yes, she understood.

'But you're not seeing it at its best, you know,' she said. 'The spring's coming and then you'll get out more and probably meet more of your neighbours.'

'They've kept themselves to themselves so far,' said Mrs Fenwick bitterly. 'And the villagers here in Stoke Dabenham look at you as if you've come from outer space!'

'Stick it out, my dear,' said Linda. 'I think you'll find you'll change your mind in time.'

'*You're* leaving,' said Sandra Fenwick. 'Mrs Perry said so!'

Not from choice, thought Linda. Oh dear no.

The baby chuckled.

'It suits *him* anyway,' said Linda, patting the child's rosy face. Mrs Fenwick looked thoughtful.

'That's the only thing,' said the girl seriously, giving him a fond hug. Then she shrugged and rose to depart.

When Linda went back to her flat at lunchtime, she found a letter from her father. She read it then sat back in silence. She was moved. Parenthood, she reflected, seemed sometimes to be the limitless capacity for sacrifice.

'... the sum we are being offered for the dairy has finally been agreed,' ran the letter. 'It is far more than we ever expected. As you know, your mum and I have our hearts set on that little bungalow at Pitsea and we've both of us agreed that we want you to have the rest to help you set yourself up into General Practice, which seems to suit you so well. Treat it as a long loan if you like, dear, but do accept. It is the way we'd be most happy to see the money used.'

She would write straight back and accept. She knew the offer was seriously meant and this would give them genuine pleasure. And she would tell them that there happened to be a partnership in a Practice going in which she was particularly interested, and she saw no reason why she shouldn't suggest herself.

I must do it while the mood is on me, thought Linda later, as she put her letter home into the village postbox. I must make the approach while I'm feeling confident. And while John Cooper is on his *own*, said her subconscious.

She walked straight back to the big house and went in to find Doctor Cooper. He was reading a newspaper in the lounge and at once invited her to sit down by the fire. Linda plunged immediately into the vital subject. He listened to her without interruption and when she had finished there was a moment of silence. Then John Cooper spoke.

'Would you really like to,' he said. 'I imagined a bright young girl like you might aim towards lusher pastures. Yes, well, let's discuss it.'

'Thank you!' said Linda, warmly. But she couldn't leave it at that. There was something she had to get a bit clearer. 'There's one point,' she began tentatively. 'I got the impression that Peter had a friend who –'

'Tom Doyle? Yes, a good fellow. But you have

established yourself here very well in these six months. I feel we could all go on working together quite satisfactorily.'

Nothing could have made Linda happier than these words, from a man whom she respected so much. Nevertheless –

'And do you think Peter will feel the same?' she pressed.

John Cooper looked thoughtful.

'You hesitate,' said Linda. 'Does that mean you think he won't?'

'Possibly,' said John Cooper, frankly. 'Not because he has any objection to you personally, believe me, nor because he's particularly set on bringing Tom Doyle in with us.'

'Then it's on professional grounds?'

'Well –'

'I know we don't always see eye to eye –'

'No, no, the point is he's had one or two awkward situations involving women doctors at the hospital. One in particular. Anyway he's developed something of a prejudice – a wariness you might say. Got it into his head that women are liable to be neurotic, irrational and to lose their head in emergencies.'

'What rubbish!' cried Linda.

'Oh, I agree,' said John Cooper, mildly.

'What unutterable nonsense!'

'Unfortunately, he's had this rather confirmed by one particular young lady. We've known her since she was a child, actually. They sail and ski together. She's an expert skier – that calls for a cool head, you'd think. Terribly fond of Peter. But there it is – she's caused him a lot of headaches. He's had to bale her out several times. At the hospital, I mean, not while sailing! Her name's Susan.'

Of course, thought Linda. What else! She was glad she knew the truth. Now she'd have no hesitation in going ahead. With no further concern for Peter's male chauvinist piggery. 'Susan' had a lot to answer for!

But if John Cooper – whose word after all was the authority in the matter – if he was prepared to accept her, then she'd make it clear she wanted to join the Practice. The two men could argue it out together. And she was putting her money on the older doctor.

Linda never knew what discussions went on between the Coopers, father and son, but when Peter officially joined the Practice, another consulting room was fitted out and Linda moved into it as the third partner.

Peter seemed to accept the arrangement without question and they remained as friendly on a personal level as they had ever been. But Linda knew he had reservations about her on the professional side. Perhaps he always would have.

Linda and Peter continued to enjoy some pleasant off-duty periods together, but they were infrequent, since Peter's time and attention were very occupied with settling in. Their professional paths did not cross for a while.

But there came the inevitable day . . .

Linda had happened to stroll into the kitchen for a word with Elsie Peach. To her astonishment she found her gingerly rubbing butter over her wrist.

'What on earth are you up to, Elsie?'

'I've just scalded myself, Doctor. I put baking soda on it but it was still hurting so –'

'So now you're all ready for the oven.'

'Well, my old mother always used to say –'

'And I'm sure it was very good advice at the time. But I think I've got something in my bag that might ease it quicker.'

'Thank you, Doctor. I didn't like to bother you when you're so busy.'

'You mustn't think like that, Elsie. I'm sure every one of the doctors here would expect you to come like any other patient. Goodness, it's really quite a bad burn. Next time anything like this happens you come running into surgery. And that's an order!'

Peter entered on her last words. 'What's an order?' he asked. 'Apricot crumble?'

'Just look at this wrist of Elsie's.'

'Heavens, that's nasty. You'd better not use that for a day or two. Rest it.'

'Thank you, Doctor. That's much more comfortable, Doctor Ford.'

Peter had seized a couple of biscuits from a tin and was making for the door again. 'Just take my advice, Elsie, and pop it in a sling.' He called back over his shoulder: 'Oh, do you think we could have lunch a twinge earlier today? I have to get off smartly. Doctor Cooper agrees.'

He disappeared.

Elsie stole a glance at Linda and the two women laughed.

'We'll all give a hand,' said Linda, and marched off in pursuit of Peter.

She found him in the lounge, where he and Doctor Cooper were talking to the vicar of the local church. Linda was about to retreat when the vicar turned to her.

'I'd be glad if Doctor Ford could stay,' he said. 'I believe she may feel concerned.'

'The vicar is a bit worried about Miss Matlock, Linda.'

'Matlock? Flora Matlock?'

'No. Her sister Harriet.'

'Harriet. I believe she's on my books, but I don't think I've ever seen her.'

'I can quite believe that,' said the vicar.

'Surely Harriet Matlock has been away from here for some time now, hasn't she?' said John Cooper.

'That's what you understood too, is it Doctor,' said

the vicar. 'Well, it's not true. She's in the house. I just caught sight of her.'

Linda was puzzled. 'So she's come back –' she began.

'The point is, her sister Flora said she wasn't there.'

'Flora Matlock's always been an odd woman,' put in Peter.

'Yes, but it was obvious I wasn't meant to have seen Harriet.'

'But why would she pretend her sister wasn't in the house when she was?' asked Linda.

'I don't know, but I have terrible misgivings. If you could have seen the look of her. Just that one glimpse I had of her at the top of the stairs. Wild and gaunt – and the expression in her eyes! Doctor, she needs medical attention, I'm sure of it.'

The vicar was looking at Linda, and she was aware that the eyes of the two other doctors were on her – waiting for her reaction.

'It's not as simple as that, Vicar,' she said cautiously. 'I can't just go barging in when nobody's asked for me.'

'I'm asking you,' said the vicar, simply.

'But why hasn't her sister Flora called me?'

'I just don't know. What I *do* know is that she is ill. I tell you if she's not been away – if she's here in the village – she'd have been to Service. Unless there is something very much amiss with her. It was a real shock to me, seeing her staring down from the landing – like a troubled spirit.'

'Could you call on her again yourself, Vicar,' said John Cooper.

'I intend to. But if she maintains this fiction that her sister isn't in the house –'

'If you could get a word from Harriet Matlock that she would like me to call –' said Linda.

'Naturally, I shall do everything *I* can,' said the vicar.

'Excuse me, I'm delaying your lunch.'

Doctor Cooper showed him out.

'Do you know anything about Flora Matlock?' asked Linda.

'Not much,' said Peter. 'She was a nurse once I believe. Prim and proper. Keeps herself to herself, and all that.' He was looking at Linda quizzically and she knew he was wondering how she'd deal with the situation. So was *she*!

That Flora Matlock was unusual, was confirmed by Elsie Peach later.

'They say she keeps the whole house sterile as an operating theatre,' said Elsie.

'You know – she's the sort who dusts the coals.'

'What about Harriet?' asked Linda, carefully.

'Her sister? Oh, she's gone away. Hasn't been seen for months.'

Linda didn't take the subject further. Some instinct advised caution in this matter of the two strange sisters.

In any case there was a sudden beating at the back door and Elsie rushed to open it. On the threshold stood a girl of about fifteen. Her skirt and jumper were snagged and her wellingtons caked with mud. Her only attempt at teenage style were a few ornaments in her black hair.

'Please! Dad's scythed 'is leg 'alf off, and we can't stop it bleedin',' she blurted out. 'Surgery door's closed an –'

'Come with me,' said Linda, and made off through the house, with the girl trotting behind her. 'When did it happen?'

''E'd just come 'ome on the tractor. Ma said to bring Doctor Cooper, 'cos she can't stop his bleedin'. She can't stop 'im yellin' either.'

'What's your name?' asked Linda.

'Polly Damerel.'

'Damerel, ah. I think you've been taken on to Doctor Peter Cooper's list, haven't you?'

'I don't know.'

'I think so. We'll just see if he's in, but if not I'll come and see your father.'

Peter wasn't in his room, so Linda grabbed her bag and steered Polly out into the yard, and into her car.

The Damerels' home was a ramshackle old cottage at the end of a rutted lane. The M.G. slithered and bounced from side to side and Linda was grateful that it wasn't a heavier car. As it was, she was sure it would get bogged down any minute. But at last they drew up at the cottage door. It opened straight into the main living room.

Linda entered, dodging nimbly under a low beam. The room was full of steam from a pan bubbling on the stove and heavy with the smell of wood-smoke.

'You've a good stew going there,' said Linda, coughing.

'Just bones for the stock, me dear,' said the woman who rose to greet her, setting aside a small child she'd been cuddling.

''Ere's the leg, Doctor.' She indicated a man sitting in the corner. ''E bled through two shirts and a pair of pants, so I thought I better send for a doctor.'

'Quite right,' said Linda, removing the dingy wrappings round the man's leg. 'How did you manage to scythe through your own leg, Mr Damerel?'

''E's done it afore, Doctor,' answered his wife. ''E's done most things afore! It's a wonder there's any blood left in 'im.'

'Plenty more where that came from,' said Linda, beginning to deal with the leg. 'But just watch one day he doesn't saw through a main artery or that'll be that!'

'See, 'Arry? Take care, will you!'

'I didn't do it a-purpose,' said her spouse, miserably.

'That's what Mr Watters thinks. The farmer 'e works

135

for, Doctor,' she added, in explanation.

'Ah,' said Linda.

''E thinks 'Arry's idea is to recline 'ere in comfort.'

Linda glanced round at the 'comfort'. The windows were cracked and their frames ill-fitting.

She had visited this cottage once before and knew it had no electricity, gas or main drainage. Yet the Damerels seemed to rub along happily enough. And Mrs Damerel was a resourceful woman.

'The baby looks very well,' said Linda, as she finished dressing the leg and rose to pack back her gear.

'My dear life, that's not the baby,' laughed Mrs Damerel. 'That's Bobby. The baby's out in the pram. And Peter 'as started school now. Just as Polly's leavin' it. She's lookin' for a job if you 'ear of somethin'.'

'Well, there's your leg, Mr Damerel,' said Linda.

'Put it on the chair, Dad,' said Polly, ministering tenderly to her father.

'We'll want to change the dressing in a couple of days,' said Linda. 'Don't forget now. It could get infected.'

Next day when Linda was enquiring after Elsie's burn, she heard more about the Matlock sisters.

'Have they lived all their lives in the village?' Linda enquired casually.

'Oh yes,' said Elsie. 'There was a bit of a palaver when Miss Flora Matlock's husband died. She was married, you know, but not that long. In fact nobody got round to calling her by her married name. He moved into the Matlock home. Poor man. They say he never set foot in the house in his shoes. And not allowed to sit on the best chairs. She dusted and cleaned and polished the spirit right out of him. In the end he was just a pair of little pale eyes. Miss Harriet was very upset at his death. Took it as hard as if she'd been married to him herself.

Felt a kindred spirit I suppose. Both of them trying to please Flora.'

'What is Harriet like?'

'Frail little woman. Very sweet. Not that I've seen her lately.'

Peter and Linda had supper together in the stable flat that evening, and Linda brought up the subject of the Matlocks.

'I know you're going to tell me not to rush in where angels –'

'Not at all,' said Peter. 'If you think there is a genuine medical problem. But if it turns out that the two old girls are just playing games with each other, you'll look a bit of a fool.'

'I'm not afraid of that side of it,' asserted Linda. 'I'm even wondering if it's a matter for the police.'

'If you're *that* worried –'

'What I think I'll do, is call at the house.'

'On what pretext?'

'I'll think of something.'

'Darling girl! The redoubtable Flora Matlock will probably eat you alive.'

'You'd better go in my place!'

'No fear.'

'By the way, you got my note about Mr Damerel's leg?'

'Yes. Thanks for coping with it for me. I'll go and take a look at him tomorrow. Draw me a map will you?'

'It's not too serious.'

Lunchtime the following day, when Linda called in at the big house, she found Peter nursing a bruise on his forehead and not in the best of moods.

'What did I *do*?' he cried in answer to her enquiry. 'Only stepped into their cottage and knocked myself unconscious! Only just stopped them sending for a doctor! You can laugh! I came to with Mrs Damerel mopping my head with some unspeakable cloth and the whole family standing round staring.'

'Were you able to dress Mr Damerel's leg?'

'Oh yes, when I could see what I was doing. The windows are too dirty to let in the light. The whole place is a complete pigsty. How the woman can raise children in it.'

'Well, she seems to have managed. And they're all fit enough.'

'I told them they've simply got to clean the place up. It's a serious health hazard!'

John Cooper had entered on Peter's last words, and Peter turned to him.

'That Damerel cottage – it's a disgrace! Something should be done!'

'Have you let off steam?' said the older man. 'Now I'm not saying conditions there are right, but I suggest you hesitate before starting any hares. It's a tied cottage, did you know?'

'And there are four children there full of mischief. It's sure to be untidy. But there's no question of neglect, I'm sure,' said Linda.

'People can't live in that fashion!'

'They don't seem to be coming to any harm.'

'So we should wait until they do?'

I've heard those words somewhere before, thought Linda.

But John Cooper was speaking to his son with some gravity.

'Peter, you can advise them and guide them – bully them a bit if you like – to try to get them to clean the place up. It'll do them no harm – in fact I doubt if it'll make the least impression. But don't be in any hurry to stir up authority.'

'It's only a matter of a little grime,' said Linda. 'If

you'd been born in the part of London where I was, you'd be used to that sort of thing. Old properties aren't easy to keep looking spotless. As long as a family is well fed and warm and loved – Whatever you say, I've never believed that cleanliness is necessarily next to Godliness!'

And that's a fact, thought Linda a few days later when to her surprise she found Flora Matlock attending her surgery with a sty on her eye.The woman was neat as a pin and had the sourest face Linda had ever seen. She was cold-voiced and spoke to Linda in a manner that was barely polite. But Linda ministered to her with the utmost care and attention, knowing that Fate had dealt her a very useful card indeed.

She left it a couple of days, then presented herself on the doorstep of Simba, the Matlocks' house, where she found herself faced across the gleaming threshold by a grim-faced Flora.

Linda gathered her courage.

'Ah, good morning, Miss Matlock. I called to see how the eye was faring.'

'Oh. I was coming to the surgery. There's no need –'

'It's no trouble at all since I was passing,' interrupted Linda, and stepped very firmly forward, so that Flora Matlock was obliged to allow her to enter or be mown down.

'What a very nice house, Miss Matlock, and how beautifully you keep it. I was brought up in an orderly home so I do appreciate it.'

Linda thought of the homey comfort of her mother's house, and felt a twinge of guilt, but she chattered on in this vein, and was gratified to observe that Flora Matlock was visibly softening – indeed beginning to simper a little with pride.

'I try to keep the place as it should be,' she said, leading the way through to an austere sitting room, where Linda went through an elaborate process of examining the sty.

'You should just see the Doctors' house sometimes, Miss Matlock. Such a muddle! What with Doctor Cooper potting his plants in the kitchen. And now young Doctor Peter is there – well – poor Elsie Peach has her work cut out keeping things straight. Of course, it's much easier for you, being on your own.'

Linda waited but Flora Matlock did not rise to the bait, instead she leant towards Linda and plucked at her shoulder.

'Excuse me – a hair,' she said, and removing it she carried it to the fire and threw it in with distaste. 'It's the only way, you know.'

'What is?' said Linda, startled.

'Burning. To destroy the germs, I mean. You'd understand, Doctor. I scald everything. You have to chase dirt every minute. The smallest corner is a breeding place. I do the front step before it's light. So much to do –'

Her eyes were shining oddly.

'You should get some help in,' said Linda, a vague idea forming at the back of her mind.

'If you want it done properly you must do it yourself. Nobody else understands. Nobody!'

Linda was making great play of packing away her equipment.

'By the way, Elsie Peach said your sister Harriet was staying in Chester.'

She could see Flora was instantly alert.

'No. Cheltenham,' she said.

'Yes, that's what *I* heard. My cousin lives there and she sent me last week's local paper. Oh, you've no need to discuss it if you'd rather not.'

'Discuss what?'

'I read about the case.' Linda had lowered her voice

and spoke sympathetically. 'I'm very sorry. Your own sister.'

'I don't understand –'

'Not very nice for you.'

'I don't know what case you're talking about, Doctor Ford, but it's nothing to do with my sister Harriet. Harriet's not in Cheltenham now. Nor was she there last week!'

'Really?' Linda made the word sound disbelieving.

'No, I say. She's here! She's been back a month!'

Linda felt a *frisson* of triumph.

'It must have been someone of the same name. I'm so glad. Your sister is here then.'

'Upstairs this very minute.'

'I'd never have guessed.' Linda made the remark sound sceptical, and at the same time moved towards the door.

At once Flora Matlock strode out into the hall and called up the stairs.

'Harriet!' she called. 'Come down here.'

Linda had stepped out behind Flora and followed her gaze up the stairs, where a figure appeared. It was a thin, pale little woman with white hair floating round her face, caught in a bun into which she was nervously pushing stray hairs.

'May I, Flora?' she said.

She came timidly down the stairs, her eyes vaguely resting on Linda, who moved towards her and took her hand.

'I'm the new doctor here, Miss Matlock. Very nice to meet you.'

At once the papery face lit up with interest.

'A young woman. How nice. I do hope you'll be happy here, my dear. It's a pretty village. At least –' She broke off and glanced at her sister, as if the statement needed Flora's approval.

'You've put that dreadful old dress on again!' Flora Matlock said angrily. 'The moths have been at it. I told you there are moths in your wardrobe, but you take no notice.'

'I scrubbed it out, Flora, just as you said. I really did.'

Flora Matlock turned to the doctor for support. 'She doesn't understand the need for hygiene. Never has. I have terrible trouble getting her to keep herself clean!'

She turned again on Harriet, who was twisting her fingers nervously and turning her head from side to side.

'And don't say you washed properly this morning because your towel was scarcely damp.'

'It's so cold in the bathroom, Flora.'

'At least go and change into a presentable dress. The grey one is fresh back from the cleaners.'

Harriet nodded and started back up the stairs, casting a single wan, polite smile back at Linda.

'She's such a trial!' said Flora Matlock. 'Not fit to be *seen*!'

It was on Linda's lips to take this matter further, but she stopped herself. She felt sure that if she was to be of any help in this situation – if she was to render the unhappy Harriet any sort of assistance – then she must not antagonise Flora. Not yet.

'In any event,' she told Peter later, 'I didn't see what I could do right then.'

'You've done all you should,' he assured her. 'The two old ladies are probably happy as bees playing this bickering game. I'll bet Harriet would be completely lost if she didn't have Flora to chase her around.'

'It's not quite like that, Peter. Flora is a fanatic and Harriet is being driven crazy by her.'

'Well – Harriet doesn't *have* to live there.'

'That's true.'

'And you are driving me crazy,' said Peter, pulling her on to his lap.

At which the conversation took a different turn.

Nevertheless Linda was able to take some action in the Matlock affair, when she managed to persuade Flora to take on Polly Damerel to help in the house. It took all her powers of cunning to talk Flora into it. And at the same time she felt the atmosphere of purity would be a useful revelation for Polly. What's more, the child would provide Linda with a spy in the Matlock camp, to report back if things worsened.

I am becoming quite Machiavellian, thought Linda, smugly.

Polly was working part-time for the Matlocks and on other days she helped Elsie Peach in the big house, so she was handy for Linda to waylay.

But the first piece of news that the girl came out with was nothing to do with the two weird sisters.

'Doctor Peter washed our blankets,' said Polly in a voice deep with admiration.

'He did *what*!'

'Last time he called,' she said, and trotted off, leaving Linda speechless.

It was something she couldn't let pass. She waited till he was in one of his particularly superior moods, then tackled him.

'You've found out, have you,' he said, turning red. 'Well, it's no big deal. I told Mrs Damerel the bedding was a disgrace. Then I realised how difficult it was for her to get that sort of thing washed – let alone dried – so I bundled it all up and brought it here. Elsie helped me do it in our machines.'

'Oh Peter!'

'Anyway, I've persuaded them to clean the place up. I left them a few packets of washing powder and a couple of bottles of bleach. What is more I'm taking up the matter of the structural condition of that cottage with the Health Officer.'

He sat back in his chair with his arms folded. Linda regarded him fondly. She had an uncertain feeling about the lengths he was taking this to, but she loved him for caring so much about the feckless Damerels. She wished she'd have seen him staggering about with those unsavoury blankets!

Three weeks passed and Polly was unaware that Linda's casual enquiries about the Matlock household held any significance. But she realised that Linda was interested in the two women, and so it was Linda she sought out at once when she had a frightening piece of news to impart.

'I don't want to stay there, Doctor Ford. I never have liked it much, but Ma said I had to as you'd got it for me and all that. But today it was awful. She found Miss Harriet had been downstairs, you see, and she was really mad! She isn't allowed down normally, see, because Miss Flora says she trails dirt and contagion round the place. She has Miss Harriet washing her bedsheets every day now. And she says her room is verminous. I don't think it's verminous, Doctor Ford.'

And there speaks an authority, thought Linda fleetingly. 'Go on, Polly,' she urged.

'She found a hairpin, you see. That's 'ow she knew Harriet had been downstairs. An' she said it was dirty an' that Miss Harriet's hair was dirty an' that she was going to come in the night and cut it off while she was sleepin'. An' Miss Harriet was cryin'. And Miss Flora was callin' her childish. She said the first thing they do in hospital is to cut your hair off because long hair's unhygienic. Do they cut your hair off, Doctor Ford?'

'No, no, no, not unless – No.'

'She locked Miss Harriet in her room and Miss Harriet was calling out that the room was closing in on her. That's when I ran away. I don't think they'd realised I was there.'

Linda didn't think so either.

'I don't want to go back,' said Polly, her eyes filling with tears.

'Of course not,' Linda reassured her. 'And don't worry about Miss Harriet, I'll do something about it.'

Shortly afterwards matters came towards a head when the vicar called to see John Cooper, and Linda found herself summoned to the lounge, where both the doctors and the vicar were sitting with serious faces.

'I've tried to get access to Miss Harriet three times this week. Each time I've been fobbed off by Flora. She's always "resting" in her room – or taking a bath or some such. Oh yes, she's admitted Harriet is in the house. But she's supposed to be poorly. Or in bed with a chill. Well, I saw her at the window one day with her face pressed against the glass!'

'What are you doing about this, Linda?' said John Cooper. 'I thought you said you'd got it in hand.'

'I've done what I could,' said Linda, lamely. 'It's difficult when Miss Harriet has not given any indication that she needs medical help. As a matter of fact I did get into the house. And I did see Miss Harriet.'

John Cooper turned to Linda in some surprise and she felt approval.

'Then you don't think there's any serious problem there?'

Linda hesitated.

'Look,' Peter interjected. 'These old biddies have got to go on living in this village. If we stir up some sort of scandal when the whole thing is just a domestic squabble. Just because Harriet hasn't been to church lately, doesn't mean Flora has her tied to the bedpost.'

'I'm sure that's not the vicar's sole concern, Peter.'

'My concern is that there is a gentle soul in that house who is suffering –'

'I believe that too!' said Linda. 'And don't worry, I'm going to tackle it.'

'Perhaps it would be best if I –' began John Cooper.

'Please leave it to me,' pleaded Linda. 'It's my case, and I should be able to find the right way to go about it. I appreciate everything you say. All of you.'

She was glad to see that her words seemed to inspire trust in the three men. And in fact the outline of a plan had been forming in her mind even as they were all talking.

As soon as surgery was over next morning, she set off on her calls. And the first one was at Simba.

Flora Matlock opened the door. She was neat as ever, but there was a strange stiffness in her and she jerked back as Linda strode straight into the hall.

'Good morning, Miss Matlock,' she said and marched straight up the stairs. After a moment's pause, Flora followed her up.

'I trust you are well yourself. The sty better? Your sister sent for me. This is her room, I believe?'

Linda turned the handle of the door that Polly had told her was occupied by Harriet.

'Sent for you?' said Flora Matlock.

'Yes. Oh dear, this door seems to be stuck. Would you, please?'

Flora gazed at her in mesmerised bewilderment. But her hand went into her pocket and she drew out a key. Linda took it, unlocked the door, entered and shut it behind her. The whole action had been a full-scale bluff. But it had worked.

Harriet was sitting on her bed, listlessly, and she complied without a word as Linda examined her. Physically she seemed to have little wrong with her, but her mental condition was clearly cause for concern. To Linda's questions, she answered in the vaguest terms. She had withdrawn into some world of her own.

Linda patted her shoulder gently, and went downstairs

to tackle Flora, who was waiting for her at the bottom of the stairs, now quite in control.

'Well?' she said.

'I've given your sister a good check-up, and I confess I can find no disease –'

'What a waste of your time then, Doctor. Typical of my sister.'

'Ah, but I do feel she is suffering from severe nervous debility, and I recommend that she has a little spell in a Nursing Home. Maycroft might be suitable –'

'It's out of the question. There's never been anything of that sort in the family.'

'Miss Harriet is quite agreeable to the idea. It's only a quiet Convalescent Home –'

'She doesn't understand. I'm quite able to care for her here. I was a nurse, you know.'

'Then you should respect my recommendation, Miss Matlock. I'll contact the Nursing Home and they'll be in touch with you.'

'Doctor Ford –'

'Your sister will be in excellent hands. You need have no fears for her. Is it still raining outside?' Linda opened the front door for herself. 'Ah, no. Everything looks brighter already.' And with a nod, she made off down the path. Her heart was beating a triumphant tattoo.

But she had not liked the malevolent expression in Flora Matlock's eyes.

'Anyway it's all arranged,' Linda was telling Peter, not without some pride. 'Unfortunately, Maycroft can't take Harriet in till next week, but then we'll have her comfortably under our eye and can decide what to do next.'

'I think you took quite a chance there,' he said. 'But it seems to have paid off.'

'Now then, don't begrudge me my little victory over that dreadful Flora.'

'Not at all. I salute you! Now you salute me – they've taken a look at the Damerels' cottage and it's as I suspected, riddled with dry rot, wet rot and an assortment of woodworm, beetles and other wildlife. Farmer Watters has got a shock coming.'

'Do you know him, Peter?'

'No.'

'Mm.'

Relaxing together that evening, Peter brought the subject up again, clearly expecting some commendation from his father. Instead the older man received the news thoughtfully.

'I only hope Watters doesn't decide he'd be better off pulling down the cottage and dispensing with Damerel's services,' he said. 'From what I hear, they're inclined to be dispensable.'

Something of this sort had crossed Linda's mind, but she was sorry to see Peter suddenly crestfallen.

'Did you have a word with Watters first?' asked John Cooper.

'No,' admitted Peter, 'I haven't seen him at all.'

As Peter walked Linda back to the stable flat later that night, she could see his jubilant mood had quite evaporated.

'Funny how different things look sometimes, when you've had a talk with the old man.'

'He's usually right.'

'Don't tell me! I guess I'd better go and have a talk with Watters. It would be about the one farmer I don't know around here!'

'He only bought the farm a year ago.'

'That figures.'

'Would you like me to speak to him?'

'You?'

'I met him at a dance. And we got on rather well.'

Peter looked at her and she could sense a confused pattern of thoughts flitting through his mind.

'There was nothing to it! But I liked him and I think I'd have no trouble putting it to him about the cottage. After all it's the Damerels we're bothered about, isn't it?'

'You're right,' said Peter. 'So, go and work your womanly wiles on Watters. Sorry, that's not fair.'

'Listen, Peter, we'll go and see Watters together. Between us we'll manage.'

'Hopefully,' said Peter, and kissed her goodnight.

He must accept that I'm right sometimes! thought Linda.

She had been feeling quite smooth since the Matlock affair. In a few days Harriet would be safely in Maycroft and she'd dealt with it all without causing a local upheaval.

Then the Matron telephoned her from Maycroft. She sounded frosty.

'You probably don't appreciate, Doctor Ford, that this is in no way a mental home.'

'I know that, but –'

'From what I hear, Miss Harriet is not at all suitable for this place.'

'What do you hear, Matron?'

'I had a long talk with her sister – Flora. She's an ex-nurse, you know.'

'Ah! I think you should be wary of anything she may have said. She may have tried to put you off.'

'Oh, not at all, Doctor. She said how Harriet was looking forward to coming and how much good she thought it would do her. It only came out in little ways about Harriet's mental condition. We really couldn't have anyone who throws their meals about, or cuts up the upholstery.'

'And Flora said Harriet did those things?'

'Not in so many words. It just came out. If anything, she was trying to play down her sister's problems.'

Linda could appreciate very well how the cunning Flora had dropped a hint here, a word there, all the time seeming to be sweetness itself, while giving the impression that Harriet's mind was disordered.

'Matron, I should have explained things more carefully to you in the first instance. Now let me tell you all about Flora and Harriet.'

Very carefully Linda told the Matron the sequence of events and when she had done the woman was as concerned and sympathetic as Linda would have wished.

'I'm glad we've cleared things up, Doctor. Don't worry, we'll have Harriet installed here in less than a fortnight.'

'Two weeks! But I thought she would be with you within a few days.'

'I'm sorry but the misunderstanding has delayed things. We took another guest into the room prepared for Harriet Matlock. But it'll only be ten days at the most –'

Linda had to be satisfied with that. And be grateful that Flora had not managed to scotch the arrangement altogether. Ten days. It wasn't so long.

Considering that there came a particularly cold snap, there was a quiet time in the surgery. John Cooper suggested that the frost had killed off all the germs. However, it did mean that Linda and Peter had a little more time to enjoy each other's company. They took some walks in the woods and spent cosy moments curled up in one another's arms by the log fire in Linda's grate. They were thus engaged one afternoon, when a call came through on Linda's telephone from Mrs. Perry.

'Doctor Ford? Is Doctor Peter there by any chance?'

'Yes,' admitted Linda, trying to sound casual.

'Thank goodness! May I speak to him. It's an

emergency, I think. I've got Polly Damerel over here.'

Peter was already at the telephone, a sixth sense alert.

'Yes, Mrs Perry? Oh God.' Peter's face contorted as he listened. 'I'll go right away.'

'What is it?' asked Linda.

'The Damerel child – one of them – What the hell did I leave that bleach with them for!'

'Oh Peter! I'm coming with you.'

Linda got the car out while Peter ran for his bag and gathered up Polly, then she drove them off at as high speed as she dared. Peter sat all the while grim-faced. She longed to speak some word of comfort to him, but until they knew for sure what had happened ... Polly meantime sat huddled in the back, giving an occasional sob.

At the Damerel cottage they were greeted by Mrs Damerel.

'Thank goodness you've come, Doctor! It's Bobby! He's poisoned, I'm sure of it!'

The two doctors rushed into the cottage where the place was in chaos. Harry Damerel was nursing Bobby on his knee while all the other children were gathered round him either crying or shouting advice. Bobby himself was scarlet in the face, screaming his head off and foaming at the mouth.

Foaming at the mouth! Almost at once, the tension in Linda's stomach eased. This was not a child in the throes of agony. This was something altogether different and if everyone would stop shouting –

'Quiet! Be quiet!' commanded Peter. The room fell silent, except for Bobby who continued to bawl loudly – bubbles foaming out of his lips.

'What do you think he's drunk,' asked Peter, beginning to examine the child. At once a chorus of contradictory information was offered to him.

'Where is the bleach I left with you?'

'It's here, Doctor,' said Mrs Damerel, producing the two bottles from under the sink. Linda took them.

'Untouched,' said Linda wryly. Peter glanced at her. He was visibly relieved.

'Has he eaten anything that might have caused this?' asked Linda. Again the room was full of helpful suggestions.

'All right,' said Peter, 'I think we may have the answer. Calm down everybody.'

He was prizing open Bobby's little hand as he was speaking and as he did so a piece of squashed soap dropped to the floor.

'I think our little friend has been making a meal of the Palmolive.'

'Bobby!' Harry Damerel shook the small boy and the bubbles flew into the air. 'Is that what you've been doin', you little monkey!'

Bobby was promptly sick. Polly and Mrs Damerel flew to his aid.

As they drove home, Linda noticed that Peter had the two bottles of bleach on the seat beside him.

'I know it wasn't that,' he said. 'But it could have been. It could easily have been. And it would have been all my fault. I've made pretty free with my advice to you, Linda. Well, maybe I'm not so smart as I thought.'

'It's not for want of caring, that's all that matters,' Linda said.

'I'll admit it, I got a bit of a shock there for a moment. I think I could use a brandy. You wouldn't happen to have –'

'Of course. Purely for medicinal purposes, of course. Come back to the fireside, my darling.'

But they had hardly stepped out of the car before John Cooper came hurrying out into the yard.

'The police have been called to the Matlocks' house,' he said.

'I'll go, Doctor Cooper,' said Linda, and swung back into her car.

She drove towards Simba full of misgivings.

At the house she found the constable and the vicar. They closed the front door behind her and then she could see what lay at the foot of the stairs. It was Flora, spreadeagled, and lying in a pool of blood. Harriet was standing nearby. The vicar was holding one of her hands in his own, in the other she held a floormop.

'I called and could get no answer,' said the vicar. 'But I could hear – noises. I brought the constable and we found Flora lying here and Harriet trying to clean up the blood.'

Even as he spoke, Harriet broke away from him and, crouching down, began swabbing the floor.

'Don't worry, Flora,' she mumbled, 'I'll get it spick and span for you. I won't let them find you all dirty like this. Not respectable. I'll clean up, Flora.'

'She's dead, Doctor,' murmured the constable, although Linda could see the woman must have been dead some hours.

'There's a shawl at the top of the stairs. She probably tripped.'

Harriet looked up, bright eyed. 'She broke the umbrella stand,' she said. 'But I've cleared up the pieces. All neat and tidy. All cleared away, Flora,' she said, addressing the dead woman.

Linda, examining the body, found her groin had been pierced by a shaft of the china umbrella stand. She had bled to death from the main artery. If Harriet had gone for help instead of setting herself to clean the place, Flora's life might have been saved. But Flora had trained her sister too well.

'May I take Miss Harriet home with me for now, Doctor?' asked the vicar. 'My wife and I will be very gentle with her.'

Harriet went with him willingly, and Linda turned her attention to the grim task before her.

I should have foreseen something like this, thought Linda. I have to accept some blame for not preventing this tragedy.

'All right, you wish you'd acted differently,' said Peter, later. 'I believe disaster was inevitable. You weren't able to stop it happening. But – as you said to me – it wasn't for want of caring.'

John Cooper said as much to her some days later, and she took heart from it. 'By the way,' the older doctor added, 'I'd particularly like you to have Sunday lunch with us this weekend.' Something in his voice alerted her. There was an odd twinkle in his eye.

'I'd love to, of course,' she said.

The twinkle rang a little warning bell, and she dressed herself with particular care. Why did she feel red was in order? Something to make her feel strong and chic and – Best get over to the big house and solve the mystery!

As Linda entered the sitting room, three figures turned towards her.

'Hello, Linda!' said Peter.

'Ah, Linda!' said John Cooper. 'Let me introduce Susan. Susan Sanders.'

I might have guessed, thought Linda.

'Susan's an old friend. Medical student. Should qualify this year. With luck, eh, Susan?'

John Cooper continued the introductions and Peter contributed pleasantries as the two young women regarded each other with polite smiles.

Susan had a fresh, outdoors air. Her skin was lightly tanned and her fair hair full of sunlight. Her body was slim, but looked powerful.

Diana – the hunter, thought Linda.

At lunch they were seated opposite each other, with

the men at either end of the table. And Linda was sharply aware of Peter's head, turning first to one woman then the other. And it seemed to her that he turned more often towards Susan. That he laughed at her jokes too much. That this whole meal was intended to convey a message to Linda. What was it? That while she herself and Peter had one sort of relationship, here was a girl who fitted more correctly into his life. The girl who he would marry. Naturally.

Linda kept up her end of the conversation with spirit – particularly considering that her heart was becoming more leaden by the minute. With the unerring instinct that women have in these circumstances, she knew without a doubt that Susan loved Peter and wanted him for her own.

Linda concentrated hard on not letting the pace of the light-hearted chat flag; on contributing to the good-humour of the occasion with some witticisms of her own. She wondered whether this duel of angels had been John Cooper's idea. She looked towards him occasionally but his expression was enigmatic. A charming smile, directed towards one woman then the other, revealed nothing.

Linda was acting her part so hard, in fact, that it came as a shock to her when a sudden silence dropped into the conversation. They were already at the coffee stage. The end of the meal. The end of everything perhaps.

But what had just been said? It was Susan who had spoken. She repeated her words.

'Peter!' she said, with a tiny edge to her voice. 'I'm asking you a question!'

'I'm sorry,' said Peter. 'Yes?'

'I said who are we crewing for this year – Harold Jolly or Charles Hedley-Smythe?'

Linda realised that the subject matter had segued into the world of yacht racing. She was lost here. This was an area of Peter's life where she had no part. She felt excluded – unimportant. And she suspected that Susan had intended as much.

But the question itself seemed simple enough, and Linda was surprised at Peter's hesitation. Until he answered.

'Susan,' he said, 'I've been meaning to tell you. I won't be sailing this summer. I'm so new to the Practice. There's too much to do.'

'But you'll have to have *some* time off,' pressed Susan.

'If I do,' said Peter, firmly, 'it won't be away from here. I've so much to learn about this place. And I'm needed.'

'But –' Susan turned her blue eyes on John Cooper. Clearly she was hoping he'd put in the right word: tell his son to enjoy his usual summer activity. He didn't.

'I'm sorry, Susan. But I'm quite sure I won't be crewing this year.'

'But, Peter, you don't have to make that sort of sacrifice just because –'

Peter laid a hand on her arm. 'Susan,' he said. 'I don't *want* to sail this summer.'

She really shouldn't have asked that question, thought Linda. And found it in her heart to be sorry for the girl, who sat pink-faced and defeated. What's more, Linda was sure that the rejection was not just a matter of the sailing, and that Susan had realised that too.

As they all dispersed, Susan held out her hand to Linda.

'Goodbye,' she said. 'I'm glad I met you.' She gave a wry little smile.

You needn't look at me like that, thought Linda. Just because you've lost, doesn't mean I've won!

Apart from her own inner feelings, Linda was more than glad that Peter was putting the Practice before personal pleasure for the time being, because it indicated a dedication that she knew would please his father, and she herself felt was necessary.

The extra doctor was helping to relieve the heavy pressure of work, which had increased dramatically when a fourth factory got into operation and its employees arrived. It was rumoured that there had been difficulties getting the complex machinery into production and long shifts were being worked throughout the day and night. This brought with it side effects – accident cases and stress problems.

Then one day Sandra Fenwick appeared again in Linda's surgery. As she had not seen her lately, Linda had believed the girl had at last adjusted to country life. Certainly she had a new and determined look in her eye, but it was not an expression that set Linda's mind at rest. She had brought in the baby for his three-in-one immunisation. The child was bouncing with health and hardly turned a hair while Linda dealt with him.

Sandra Fenwick thanked Linda politely and rose to go.

'Are you feeling more settled now, Mrs Fenwick?' asked Linda, looking at the girl closely. 'Are you beginning to enjoy your surroundings a little more now?'

'Hardly,' replied the girl. 'In fact I've come to the conclusion that one way and another there's no point in me staying.'

'Sit down,' said Linda. 'What do you mean?'

Sandra Fenwick hesitated, then she returned to her seat and told Linda her plans. It appeared that Jim, her husband, was spending more hours at work than in his home. And when indoors, he was more often than not asleep with fatigue. And her neighbours seemed fully occupied with the decoration of their new homes. She had reached the stage where the lonely dark winter days had got the better of her and she was leaving Jim at the end of the month and going back to live with her mother.

'It's all arranged,' concluded Sandra Fenwick.

'I'm sorry to hear it,' said Linda.

Mrs Fenwick dropped her eyes, but her jaw was set in a stubborn line.

'Will you do me a favour?' asked Linda.

The girl looked up at her enquiringly.

'During your last few days here, get out in the woods and take a look at things.'

'There's nothing to see.'

'There are lambs already up at Barnett's Farm.'

Linda felt inadequately equipped to explain what she instinctively felt the rural life had to offer, for wasn't she herself still supremely ignorant on country matters?

In this respect she felt jealous of Peter's knowledge of things that were to her still mysteries, hedged about with unexpected custom or necessity.

There was the day when she'd omitted to walk through the disinfectant bath when entering a farm where Foot and Mouth disease was suspected. Peter had certainly made the point clear to her!

And when one of the farmers had shot a rather attractive stray dog, she'd felt terribly angry. But Peter saw it with a countryman's eyes. You can't have dogs running loose on farmland. They have to be kept under control as much as in town. She'd had quite a row with Peter that time but in the end she came a little nearer to understanding his argument, particularly when she'd seen six ewes in lamb with their throats ripped out.

Living close to nature did have a harsh side which could astonish a townsman.

Poor Sandra Fenwick could see only the hostility and indifference around her. It bothered Linda and she brought the subject up a few days later when she and Peter were having a relaxing lunch together.

John Cooper had gone to a sherry party and she had

suggested that Peter join her at the stable flat. Now they were both enjoying roast beef, baked potatoes and sprouts.

But Peter's view was less than sympathetic towards Sandra Fenwick.

'So she's going off and leaving her husband flat when he most needs her, is she?' he said, stabbing at another potato.

'I'm not saying it's a great idea,' said Linda. 'But I can understand a little of how the girl feels. Everything's come up to boiling pitch with her. It is at that sort of climax in our life that we reveal our true character. There's a build up to a flashpoint of tension and out come our basic qualities or defects. I can't condemn the girl so totally.'

'That's because you're a woman. You're regarding it on a purely emotional level. What about the poor husband's supper? Who's to cook it? Did you say there were more sprouts?'

Linda passed him the vegetable dish.

'You mean men never get emotional?' said Linda, looking at him sideways.

'They're more objective,' went on Peter. 'Now take these baked potatoes. I think they're marvellous, but I don't say "My word she cooked them specially for me, she's in love with me". Or if they'd been revolting I wouldn't think "She's seeking to ruin my digestion and damage my professional career". No, as a man, I view these potatoes with detachment and say "This woman is an excellent cook", and that's that!'

Linda snorted.

'No,' said Peter calmly, 'I think your patient Mrs Fenwick has met her testing time and reacted with typical feminine lack of logic, reason and common sense.'

'What a diabolically ridiculous and smug statement!' shouted Linda, smacking down her knife and fork.

'You see, you prove my point,' said Peter with infuriating calm. 'At once a wild defensive reaction.'

'Defensive nothing!' cried Linda. 'I'm going to demolish your argument, believe me!'

'I doubt it,' said Peter.

The telephone rang.

'Saved by the bell!' he added, jauntily.

Linda lifted the receiver. Almost before she could speak a voice was gabbling at her urgently. Linda listened with growing alarm.

'We're coming!' she said. 'At once!'

Seeing her face, Peter rose and came over. She put down the receiver.

'We must get over to the new factories, right away. There's been an explosion at the marine engineering works,' she said. 'Part of the building has collapsed and there are workmen trapped.'

She crossed the room and collected her case, as Peter made for the door.

'The engineering works?' he said. 'That's the one with the clock tower?'

'Yes,' said Linda, 'this side of the housing estate – but there are fire engines there and a whole block is involved. I don't think we'll miss it,' she said grimly.

The two doctors ran across to the surgery for medical equipment, then to their cars. Peter's BMW shot ahead and Linda soon lost sight of him amongst several other cars that were headed to the scene of the disaster.

The dust had not yet settled over the rubble that spilled down from the side of the building, exposing gaping holes and jutting girders where had been a three-storey factory section. Here and there were tongues of flame and firemen were tackling these, whilst others were digging and hauling away hunks of masonry.

Already there were numbers of people gathered and frantic groups were clearing piles of bricks, in an attempt to release their workmates who were trapped below.

Two men were carrying a stretcher towards an ambulance and Linda could see another victim being lifted from the wreckage. She clambered over the crumbling mountain towards the spot.

'I'm a doctor,' she said.

'Thank God,' said a worried fireman. 'Can you give this poor devil a shot?'

Linda bent over the mutilated figure and administered a merciful injection.

'How many people are in here?' she asked.

'About twenty. But there are some unharmed but trapped through there.' He pointed. 'They're cutting a way to them.'

Linda picked her way deeper into the remains of the building. She caught sight of Peter kneeling beside a man with a gash in his head. And then she spotted John Cooper. Someone must have contacted him, and he'd come from his party. He was half hidden in a knot of firemen, and his coat was off. She could see his back straining at something.

A group of men were pulling away a shattered door. They beckoned her over and she quickly hurried to their side. They had found someone. But he was dead. Linda confirmed this, and moved on.

A fireman grabbed her arm and guided her urgently down a corridor to an opening in a wall.

'There's a chap in there,' he said. 'He sounds pretty groggy. We can't get him out yet, but they're cutting through as fast as they can. Can you help him?'

Linda began to climb into the hole.

'Wait, miss,' said the fireman. 'I ought to warn you, that wall could collapse at any moment.'

'I understand,' said Linda.

Flat on her stomach she eased her slim body through.

When she reached the man, Linda found he was

trapped by the legs. He did not seem to be in pain but was badly shocked. He grasped her hand gratefully.

An hour later they were still incarcerated. The sound of hacking and drilling came from above and an occasional alarming fall of dust.

The minutes passed. Linda and the man talked. About their jobs, about what had caused the explosion. Anything. It helped.

A voice called in to tell them that all the others had been rescued and to keep their spirits up as all efforts were now centred on this part. But time went by. The noises got nearer and louder, and at one point a beam crashed down close by.

Then from the opening of the tunnel Linda suddenly heard Peter's voice.

'Linda!' he called, urgently. 'Come out of there. I'll take over.'

'No,' said Linda. 'We're O.K.'

'It's dangerous!' His voice was a tone higher.

'It's all right!' said Linda sharply, hearing an intake of breath from the man beside her.

'I'm coming through to get you out!'

Linda heard a fall of debris. Her heart pounded. Suppose he disturbed some vital support and brought the whole structure down!

'Don't be a fool, Peter!' Why was he endangering another life? What could she say to stop him. 'Get back!' she commanded. 'You may be needed!'

Her words brought Peter to a halt and she heard him clambering back to safety. She sighed with relief.

Linda and the man were released twenty minutes later. She followed the stretcher as they carried him out into the daylight.

A woman ran forward and threw her arms round him, sobbing.

'Jim!' she cried. 'Oh, Jim dear!'

It was Sandra Fenwick.

As Linda walked off John Cooper intercepted her. He placed his hand on her shoulder and gripped it warmly. He did not need to speak.

She moved wearily to her car. Peter was standing beside it. He looked very shaken.

'You didn't have to go to such lengths to explode my theory,' he said.

'What? What did you say?'

Peter had opened the door of his car and was helping her in.

'My car –' began Linda.

'The police will bring it. Right now I'm driving you home.'

'Are you sure you yourself –'

'Don't rub it in,' said Peter ruefully. 'I tell you, I accept that women are capable of staying cool in a crisis; and that men are capable of losing their heads. Some are anyway!'

Linda smiled, and felt the dust crack on her face.

'I was glad you were nearby,' she said.

Peter suddenly gathered her in his arms and buried his face against her shoulder.

'Oh, darling, I've never felt so worried in my whole life. I was sure the building would fall and you'd be killed. It was a nightmare. To have lost you!'

Linda stroked his hair and held him close.

'And you were wonderful,' he added. 'I admired you so much. I suppose I always have really. I always suspected you had guts. But I thought it was just because I loved you that I was giving you more credit than other women. That maybe I was seeing you in a rose-coloured spotlight!'

He was cleaning her face gently with his handkerchief as he talked. 'I admit totally that I very nearly made a complete fool of myself out there. Not entirely mind – but I certainly could have.'

Linda smiled. 'You see how people can behave when they're –' She stopped short.

'I guess anybody at all can lose their wits in an emergency. But in my case, of course, there were mitigating circumstances.'

She looked up into his face and what she saw was as delightful as ever. But there was something new as well. A kind of calm satisfaction.

It was as if something important had been settled. Another sort of wall has crumbled away today, thought Linda.

Three weeks later, Linda visited the new housing estate to call on Jim Fenwick, whose legs were making a slow but definite recovery.

Sandra Fenwick took her through to the living room where her husband was sitting. She looked very pretty.

'You're still here, then,' said Linda, smiling at her.

'Look!' said the girl. She pointed to a table laden with fruit and flowers and get-well cards. 'From the neighbours and people in the village.' Her eyes were suddenly filled with happy tears. 'They've been absolutely wonderful. I think I've made some real friends.'

'I'm so very glad,' said Linda.

'So am I!' said Jim Fenwick, with an affectionate grin at his wife.

'And Doctor,' said Sandra Fenwick, awkwardly. 'I did as you said. Have you seen? The hedges are covered with green buds. Doesn't Spring happen suddenly here? It'll be our first in the country.'

Mine too, thought Linda. And wondered what the burgeoning year held for *her*.

She drove back slowly along the quiet lanes beside the rust red fields waiting to be warmed into new life.

Like the sweet seed that had now so surely been sown in her heart. Peter loved her and wanted her for always. She'd read it in his eyes. He knew as well as she did that they belonged together. And one day soon, she knew without a doubt, that he would tell her so.

ABOUT THE AUTHOR

Jean McConnell is a prolific writer of plays, television and radio scripts, and short stories. Her stories have appeared in anthologies and magazines worldwide. For television she has written for the BBC (including the popular BBC medical drama Dr Finlay's Casebook), Granada and channels in the USA and Europe. Jean's radio plays have been heard on the BBC and in Germany and Zambia. Her plays have been performed in theatres around the UK and internationally. She is a member of the Crime Writers' Association and a Vice President of the Society of Women Writers and Journalists.

Printed in Great Britain
by Amazon.co.uk, Ltd.,
Marston Gate.